ALSO BY THOMAS PRIDE

Fever

Mercia

King and Country

Wonderful Untouchables

Zayed

The Baron

THOMAS PRIDE

Ucadia Books Company

Published by Ucadia Books Company, a Delaware stock corporation (File Number 6779670) 901 N Market St #705 Wilmington Delaware 19801.
First edition.

Thomas Pride is the pen name and true ancestor of an Australian based philosopher and writer.

ISBN 978-1-64419-003-6

Hero or villain?

Few real military and political figures are more enigmatic than Baron Roman Nikolai Maximilian von Ungern-Sternberg. Borne into an ancient and wealthy Austrian-Estonian aristocratic family. Awarded for his heroic efforts at the age of 18 in the Russo-Japanese War 1904-05, the Baron rejected his heritage, joining the ranks of the famous Cossacks and served on the front lines with the 34th Regiment, receiving more awards for his bravery and leadership. After the Bolshevik-led October Revolution of 1917, he became a key commander of the White Russian resistance to the communists and their Red Army.

By 1920, the Baron was commissioned to form the Asiatic Cavalry Division of more than 6,000 Christian, Muslim, Buddhist, Jewish and Hindu soldiers from more than 30 diverse tribes and cultures. Yet so threatened were the communists by the Baron that virtually the whole Red Army was sent to destroy him.

No figure in Soviet folklore is more condemned than the Baron Roman Nikolai Maximilian von Ungern-Sternberg. Today, thanks to Soviet authors and popular socialist culture, the Baron is remembered as an insane psychopath, a modern-version of Vlad the Impaler (Dracula) and a wicked soul, to be feared as the "Bloody Baron".

To all those who never surrendered to propaganda and lies.

Be who you are and say what you feel, because those who mind don't matter and those who matter don't mind.

Dr. Seuss

Chapter 1

Against the breathtaking backdrop of snow capped mountains and sweeping fields of grasslands, a solitary train steamed along the Trans-Siberian line. An odd assortment of carriages - a mix of freight and passenger cars of different classes, interspersed with flat bed trays supporting machine gun nests, protected by sand bags. An Imperial Crest adorned the front of the locomotive, accentuated on either side by two oversized Imperial Russian flags. In the distance, the crystallising mirage of an approaching city.

Alone inside a first class cabin, a young handsome Imperial Russian officer (Baron Ungern-Stenberg), in the colours of the Amur Cossacks, stared blankly out of the window at the passing landscape; lost for a moment in his own thoughts, whilst tapping a ring on the rim of the window slowly in time with the rhythm of the train as it *clickity-clacked* along the tracks. He stopped the tapping, before resting his feet onto the seat opposite, slouching down into his own seat and closing his eyes to sleep.

Except, there was no escape to any peace called sleep. Instead, his eyelids barely hide the inner turmoil of grotesque and inhuman remembrances of hand to hand combat against Japanese foes; and of blood, smoke and screams of battle. The whizzing of bullets as they zing past; and the utter exhaustion of fight-or-die; and the ferocity of the historic 1904 battle of Port Arthur unfolding with relentless inevitability.

The Baron awoke from the nightmares upon the slowing of the train. Through the train window he could see the outskirts of the city pass by - images of peasants with horses and carts moving along a dirt road next to the rail line, to the image of small factories and buildings, to the imposing image of half a dozen Cossacks on their horses with their rifles, eyeballing the slowing train as it trundled past them.

****

Blagoveshchensk Station, Amur Region, East Siberia 1912

Chapter 1

The train came to a stop at a quaint train station, guarded by more Cossacks, pulling up next to a stationary train pointing in the opposite direction, festooned with Buddhist flags and symbols.

As soon as the train finally stopped, a flurry of activity ensued as porters rushed to open doors and unload baggage and soldiers moved into position to cordon off the front of the train from the people travelling at the back.

Midst the activity, Baron Ungern-Sternberg stepped out of his cabin and onto the platform, carrying his rifle and sack. He immediately looked to the back of the train where porters had started to off load some horses.

At the same time, on the station platform opposite, an elderly well dressed man with distinct Mongolian features (Namnansuren), watched the activity with a wry smile. Next to him, a large burly looking Cossack Officer (Semyonov) and two other Cossack soldiers (Rezukhin and Veselovskii) also looked on.

As the porters wrestled with offloading a particularly spirited horse, Rezukhin spotted and then pointed out the Baron to Semyonov and Veselovskii.

The Baron

They observed as the Baron at first argued with the porters until they handed him the reigns. The soldiers watching on the opposite platform started to laugh loudly to one another at the commotion, until they witnessed the Baron slowly settle the horse down. Hearing the laughter, the Baron looked over at the platform opposite.

"You are too late!" yelled Semyonov to the Baron.

The Baron shrugged his shoulders and then cupped his hand against his ear, yelling back at Semyonov.

"What did you say?"

The Baron steadied his horse down a ramp from the platform and across the tracks to the edge of the platform opposite where Semyonov and the Cossack soldiers were still standing with Namnansuren watching the unfolding events.

At that moment, the Baron was transfixed as a stunningly beautiful young woman in traditional Mongolian dress (Erdene), accompanied by a thin and officious looking man (Damdini Sukhbaatar) appeared on the platform. She briefly locked eyes with the Baron and allowed him the briefest smile.

"I said you're Late," grinned Semyonov at the Baron. "The Parade was last month."

Chapter 1

Chuckles and laughter rang out among the Cossacks, as the Baron, still holding his horse, remained transfixed at the sight of Erdene now standing next to Namnansuren, oblivious to the comments aimed at him by Semyonov.

"I am Baron Roman Nikolai Maximilian von Ungern-Sternberg," smiled the Baron to Erdene, before Namnansuren stepped in front of Erdene, blocking her eye contact with the Baron.

"And I am Namnansuren Khan," responded Namnansuren angrily. "The Ruler of Sain Noyon and Prime Minister of Outer Mongolia."

The Baron bowed deeply to Namnansuren before looking up and watching as three more Mongolian guards accompanying another official looking Mongolian man in a suit (Mijiddorjiyn Handdorj), marched over to Namnansuren. A seeming eternity of awkwardness passed as the Baron dared not lift his head again from his bow of respect.

As soon as he heard the sound of shuffling feet, the Baron lifted his head to the surprise of seeing Erdene still standing with Damdini Sukhbaatar in the same spot though Namnansuren, Mijiddorjiyn Handdorj and their guards had gone.

The Baron

Erdene paused, looking at the Baron a moment longer before Damdini Sukhbaatar tapped her on the shoulder. She ignored Damdini Sukhbaatar for a second, then bowed to the Baron, who bowed to her in return, before Erdene turned and departed, ignoring Damdini Sukhbaatar altogether. Damndini Sukhbaatar then locked eyes on the Baron for a moment, snarling at him, before swivelling on his heals to chase after Erdene and the rest of the Mongolian party.

"You certainly made a lasting impression by staring at his daughter," chuckled Semyonov.

More laughter from the two other Cossacks as Semyonov stepped down from the platform to the Baron. Semyonov extended his hand to the Baron.

"Grigory Mikhaylovich Semyonov."

The Baron shook his hand. "She is the most beautiful creature I have ever seen," he replied. "What is her name?"

Semyonov slapped the back of the Baron as he continued to keep grip of the reigns of his horse.

"And that is the closest you will ever get to see her my friend," grinned Semyonov. "Her name is Erdene and her train leaves within the hour to Irkutsk where we will leave them."

Chapter 1

Semyonov looked at his watch and then at the Baron, slapping the arm of the Baron this time.

"I still have time," smiled Semyonov. "Come, let me introduce you to the Colonel."

Semyonov signalled to Veselovskii to come down off the platform to where Semyonov and the Baron were standing.

"Stepan Borisovich will take good care of your horse for you."

The Baron nodded and handed Veselovskii the reigns and then turned to catch up with Semyonov who was already marching away.

"I am sorry Grigory Mikhaylovich," said the Baron, "I did not introduce myself. I am Baron Roman Nikolai Maximilian von Ungern-Sternberg."

"I know," said Semyonov.

****

Semyonov and the Baron salute the guards out the front of the Cossack headquarters and march inside.

Inside an office within the building, a Colonel (Yahiv Kukharenko) was busily signing page after page of a pile of papers until the knock on the door.

"Enter," barked the Colonel.

The Baron

Semyonov and the Baron stepped into the office and salute the Colonel. The Colonel looked at Semyonov and then the Baron and slapped his own forehead.

"Captain, why aren't you on a train with the Mongolians?" sighed the Colonel.

Semyonov looked at the Baron and then back to the Colonel. "Colonel. My new Lieutenant has arrived, so I -"

"Damn it Semyonov. I am babysitting the Prime Minister of Outer Mongolia and his delegation and the Chinese and their delegation and until they leave safely I have General Suvorov the Commander In Chief for the District on my neck and then you go and do this to me -"

"Lieutenant Ungern-Sternberg reporting," interrupted the Baron.

"Yes, I know who you are Baron," replied the Colonel dryly. "I know all about your exploits during the war with the Japanese and Americans. But that doesn't change the fact that Semyonov disobeyed a direct -"

"Begging your pardon Colonel," interrupted Semyonov. "But it was my idea. You see I request to accompany the Captain on his assignment sir."

Chapter 1

Semyonov looked at the Baron and then back to the Colonel as the Colonel continued to shake his head.

"Doesn't anyone follow orders around here?" moaned the Colonel. "I mean, sure why not take a vote?"

"It will give me time get him up to speed," replied Semyonov.

The Colonel puts his hands over his head and looked down. "Very well. Go GO!" yelled the Colonel, "and if you miss that train, then I will have BOTH OF YOU arrested and court marshalled."

Semyonov and the Baron saluted, turned and quickly exited the office.

****

Semyonov and the Baron walk quickly back along the street toward the Train Station.

"Why did you do that?" asked the Baron. "He could have had you arrested and shot?"

"Don't worry about him. He is from the academy. All Bark. Not like a real soldier's soldier. Besides, I made a bet with the other men you will fail to speak to the princess."

"Oh, I will get to speak with her."

The Baron

Within sight of the Station, they hear the sound of the train engine whistle, signalling its departure.

"Not if we miss THAT train," yelled Semyonov, as both men break into a sprint for it.

Both men close the final yards to the train as the carriages groan and wheels squeal into motion, with Semyonov the first to get alongside. He managed to grab hold of the side rail of a carriage and swing himself onto the train, as it continues to pick up speed. Yet the Baron was not as quick.

By the time the Baron came alongside, only four carriages remained as the train continued to accelerate past him. From behind him, the Baron heard shouting from the last carriage, a stock car with its side door open and several Cossacks yelling encouragement. The Baron turned around while still running to see Rezukhin leaning out of the carriage, held by Veselovskii to try and grab him.

Just at the last carriage was about to pass, Rezukhin grabs the arm of the Baron and hauls him unceremoniously up onto the train.

****

Chapter 1

Semyonov and the Baron relax in one of the Cossack carriages with Rezukhin, Veselovskii and other soldiers, drinking and laughing. Semyonov pointed to a patch of blood on the left trouser of the uniform of the Baron.

"I see you may have a memento of our first adventure Baron?"

The Baron looked down at a blood spot just below his knee and rolled up his trouser to reveal a bloody gash to a collective "ah" and more laughing in the carriage.

"Now you are a real Cossack!" declared Rezukhin.

"I will get a needle and thread comrade," added Semyonov.

"No need," smiled the Baron, "It is not that deep."

On queue, as if the sight of blood represented to bored soldiers the opening of some beauty pageant for scars, one by one the Cossaks in the carriage began rolling up their shirt sleeves and trousers to reveal various scars to more "ahs" from the rest of the soldiers.

"Comrade, it is but a paper cut," boasted Veselovskii at the sight of a scar on the side of the neck of one of the soldiers. "Let me show you the memory of the last man who tried to kill me."

The Baron

Veselovskii unfurled his shirt to reveal a deep scar on his left side of his rib cage, extending around to his abdomen. As more "ahs" echoed around the carriage none of the Cossacks at first noticed that the Baron had completely unbuttoned his shirt to reveal the unmistakable scars of bullets to his upper arm and side. When they noticed, the carriage went eerily silent, at the sight of a clear winner.

"The Battle of Port Arthur?" asked Semyonov, almost reverently to the Baron.

The Baron nodded affirmatively as he slid his shirt back on and started to re-button it. One by one the Cossacks moved forward and slapped him on the back.

"You are a real Cossack!" declared Veselovskii.

Collective laughing and then clinking of bottles return to the carriage, as the connecting door toward the first class cabins opened and an officer in the uniform of a US Army Captain (Elmore Taggart) appeared, holding more bottles of alcohol.

"I hope I am not interrupting?" he smiled.

Semyonov signalled for him to step in. Behind him was a second officer in the uniform of a French major (Maurice Janin), smoking a cigarette and then a British officer in a major's uniform (Edmund Ironside).

Chapter 1

Ironside looked around at the empty bottles littering the floor and shook his head.

"What a bloody mess!" he grumbled.

As the foreign officers moved forward, two Cossacks quickly cleared the table of bottles, then placed a blanket over it, re-arranging the chairs. Semyonov signalled for the foreign officers to take a seat. Captain Taggart looked over at the bunks along the side of the carriage and the Baron laying down, while Taggart removed two decks of cards from his pocket, placing them on the table.

"You're new," said Taggart, eyeballing at the Baron. Taggart looked at Semyonov. "Who is this?"

The Baron sat up from the bunk and moved over to Taggart to shake his hand.

"I am Baron Roman Nikolai Maximilian von Ungern-Sternberg."

"Royalty! Good for you then," chimed Ironside, shaking the hand of the Baron. "I am William Edmund Ironside and if we are not going to have a game of it, then I will have to go back and drown my sorrows on this excellent vodka."

"This is Major Edmund Ironside," added Semyonov, looking at the Baron. "Don't worry. He is a British spy."

The Baron

"Manners Grigory -" huffed Ironside, looking upset that the obvious had even been spoken.

General laughter again rippled through the carriage as Semyonov grabbed the shoulder of the Baron - moving him in front of Maurice Janin, who bowed before shaking his hand.

"And this is French Major Maurice Janin," said Semyonov. "I don't think he is a spy as he is too busy stealing antiques."

Semyonov then pointed to Elmore Taggart.

"And this man is the American Captain Taggart and a rotten card shark with the American Trading Co. and -"

"Hey, lay off the compliments Semyonov," responded Taggart sarcastically. "Can we just play cards?"

Semyonov then sat down at the fourth chair as the Baron and the rest of the men watched on.

****

A ghostly silhouette enveloped the train, against the backdrop of a perfectly clear moonlit night sky, as it continued its journey.

Chapter 1

Inside the Cossack carriage, the air was even thicker with smoke as the card game continued. In front of the American Captain Elmore Taggart sat a huge pile of gold coins, with a modest pile each in front of the British Major Edmund Ironside and the French Major Maurice Janin. But in front of Semyonov were only three gold coins. At the centre of the table, sat a pot of several dozen gold coins.

"All or nothing comrades!"

With that, Semyonov slapped down his cards onto the table and pushed his final three coins into the pot, while the three other players glanced briefly at each other and then back at the stony faced Semyonov.

"Well I guess this is it my friend," grinned Elmore Taggart, pushing nine coins into the pot from his great bounty. "Show me."

Semyonov reluctantly rolled over his cards to the others, revealing he had nothing. A moment later French Major Maurice Janin and British Major Edmund Ironside followed, as Taggart displayed his winning cards to a collective sigh.

"What fiendish craft is this you Americans have?" moaned Edmund Ironside.

The Baron

Semyonov slowly picked himself up from his seat and moved over to the Baron, who was still awake, reading a book using a small pen light.

"Baron, we have a spare chair," said Taggart.

The Baron looked up from his book at the three officers still sitting at the table like three crows sitting on a gallows waiting for the next condemned man. Semyonov tilted his head so he could read the title on the cover.

"What is he reading?" asked Maurice Janin.

"The Strategies of Ghengis Khan," replied Semyonov to muffled laughter.

"You'd be right at home with Alexandre," added Maurice Janin. "He's a bookworm like you."

"Who?" asked the Baron.

"Alexandre Miller. The Russian Consul in the other carriage," replied Semyonov. "He thinks card games are beneath him."

"Are you going to play or what?" interrupted Taggart, clearly annoyed they were losing valuable gambling time to chatter.

"I think our American friend here thinks you are a *real* Baron with real money," responded Edmund Ironside.

Chapter 1

"I *am* a real Baron with German, Austrian and Estonian family titles," growled the Baron as he threw down his book and sat up.

"I am confounded," said Maurice Janin, "Why on earth would a man of your title then join the Cossacks, much less be on this train in the middle of nowhere?"

"He is more interested in the princess," grinned Semyonov to more laughter as the Baron scowled at him

"Ah voilà!" said Maurice Janin. "It all makes sense then. Very well. If you win, I shall introduce you."

The Baron looked back at Semyonov and then at the three officers sitting at the table, before striding over and sitting down at the spare chair.

****

The carriage was now quiet, as soldiers were sleeping and snoring, including Semyonov, except for the Baron and the three foreign soldiers who continued to play cards. During the relatively short passage of time, fortunes had changed considerably. On the table in front of the American Captain and British Major rested a handful of coins each, with the Baron having amassed himself a treasure. Only French Major

The Baron

Maurice Janin possessed a modest sum of coins compared to the Baron.

"You know war is coming," said Maurice Janin to the Baron.

Both Taggart and Ironside quickly turn their attention to the Frenchman and scowl.

"The man is reading military strategy for goodness sake," responded Edmund Ironside sarcastically, as Maurice Janin shrugged his shoulders.

"Yes, but I -"

"I know," interjected the Baron.

"Well Baron, it is going to be a slaughter," added Edmund Ironside. "Best you find yourself a good field commander with real experience and don't do anything fool-"

"If I may," interrupted Maurice Janin, sounding frustrated, "What I meant was that with war coming, what will the Baron do? As Germany and the Austrian-Hungarian Empire are more than likely to be enemies of Imperial Russia and Great Britain!"

"My heart is with Russia," replied the Baron.

"Bon chagrin!" exclaimed the Frenchman, "A Romantic as well!"

At that moment, Maurice Janin pushed his entire pile of coins into the central pot. The Baron looked at him and smiled, pushing his entire pile of coins into the centre.

"That is more my style Baron," said Elmore Taggart. "Now we have a good old fashioned stand off."

The Baron and the Frenchman stare at each other, neither flinching, until, finally Maurice Janin sighed and threw in his cards.

"Well played Monsieur. What did you have?"

The Baron revealed his cards to the three foreign officers. He held nothing.

"Excellent bluff Baron," smiled Edmund Ironside. "Now it is time for Maurice to honour his promise."

****

The 1st class carriage was quiet, with people either sleeping or reading. On one double seat was Alexandre Miller, busily reading, as Maurice Janin, followed by the Baron and then Edmund Ironside and Elmore Taggart entered the carriage. Alexandre Miller looked up when he spotted Maurice Janin.

"Enjoyed your games?"

Maurice Janin and the Baron stop in front of where Alexandre Miller was sitting as the Baron deciphers the title of the book Miller was holding. It was *Carl von*

The Baron

Clausewitz - Philosophy of War but in German. Alexandre Miller briefly looked up at the Lieutenant's uniform of the Baron and allows himself a wry superior smile.

"Alexandre," said Maurice Janin, "meet Baron von Ungern-Sternberg. Baron, meet the Russian Consul to Outer Mongolia."

The Baron extended his hand and Alexandre Miller shook politely, before returning to reading his book. Maurice Janin shrugged his shoulders before nodding and walking away to the door at the opposite end of the carriage and then opening the door to leave.

"Clausewitz is a complete waste of time," said the Baron dryly. "Von Clausewitz only works if both sides believe economic might alone wins a war. But all it takes is one brilliant general and the will to win."

Alexandre Miller stopped reading and looked up and glared at the Baron, before a brief laugh erupted from Elmore Taggart standing behind with Edmund Ironside.

"Here we go," whispered Taggart to Ironside.

"You read German? And that is your *expert* opinion Baron?" replied Alexandre Miller.

The Baron smiled. "German, French, Russian, English, Hungarian and Estonian."

Chapter 1

"It is true," added Taggart enthusiastically. "He *really* is a Baron."

Alexandre Miller rubbed his chin and then closed his book, before looking back up at the Baron and nodded his head.

"Ah yes, I have heard of you," said Alexandre Miller. "I remember hearing a story about a young aristocrat who went to join the fighting at Port Arthur. A real hero, who then flatly turned down a diplomatic post after the War with Japan, instead choosing to join the Pavlovskoe Military School in St. Petersburg as an ordinary cadet."

The Baron nodded his head. "Yes."

Alexandre Miller let out a brief laugh. "I am sorry Baron von Ungern-Sternberg. I did not mean to be impolite. I always thought the stories were fiction or propaganda at best. You know, the elite consider you to be completely mad. But now having met you, I can say -"

Alexandre Miller stopped mid sentence as everyone was staring behind the Baron. The Baron swung around to see at first the beaming face of Maurice Janin and then the beautiful smiling face of Erdene.

"We meet again," said Erdene softly.

The Baron

For a moment, the Baron was tongue tied as Maurice Janin starts laughing.

"Monsieur. After what it has cost me at cards, surely you thought of something to say?"

"I hope your father will forgive me if I caused any offence," said the Baron.

"I cannot speak for my father, but I am happy to again meet you."

The Baron smiled broadly at Erdene as Erdene also continued to smile at him. Maurice Janin waved his hand at the Baron to gain his attention.

"Monsieur. Maybe you wish some privacy to continue your conversation in the dining cabin?"

The Baron nodded then looked to Erdene who also noded approvingly. Yet, as soon as Erdene turned to leave the carriage followed by the Baron, Damdini Sukhbaatar burst into the carriage, followed by Namnansuren dressed in his official Mongolian Court clothes and hat.

Namnansuren scowled as he locked eyes with the Baron as Damdini Sukhbaatar stepped to one side to allow him to pass.

"Return to our carriage at once," shouted Namnansuren to Erdene.

Chapter 1

"But father, the carriage is full of people. I was only
-"

"Do as I request. If not as your father, then as steward of our people."

Erdene bowed and briefly glanced back at the Baron before leaving. Namnansuren pressed forward to stand defiantly in front of the Baron. The Baron bowed in respect.

"Your Highness, I am sorry if I -"

"I cannot force you off this train, as I remain a guest of Russian hospitality. But I forbid you from ever speaking to my daughter again."

Namnansuren turned and walked out of the carriage followed by Damdini Sukhbaatar who gave the Baron one last look of disgust.

For a moment, the Baron remained standing and staring toward the end of the carriage, as if Erdene was still standing there, before Alexandre Miller came up behind and patted him gently on the shoulder.

"I hope you are a better soldier than you are a diplomat?"

****

Irkutsk Train Station

The Baron

The train stopped at the Irkutsk Station as the Cossack guards patrol the platform and around the train. The Baron stood at the opposite end of the platform to the first class carriages as he watched the Mongolian Delegation and Erdene depart. Semyonov walked up behind the Baron.

"A dream comrade. Nothing more," said Semyonov. "Let it go."

The Baron ignored Semyonov and continued watching and staring in the hope Erdene might look sideways in his direction. A moment and then another before she disappeared, never turning.

Only when the last Mongolian guards were out of view did the Baron turn around to Semyonov and speak. "If I am not the master of my own dreams, then what kind of man am I?"

Chapter 2

Cossack Headquarters, Blagoveshchensk

The Baron walked alone to the entrance of the Cossack Headquarters at Blagoveshchensk. He exchanged salutes with the guards before entering the building.

Inside, within the office of Colonel Kukharenko, the Colonel was again signing and flinging papers at a hapless soldier, standing next to his desk. The Colonel finished signing a document, before flicking it to the soldier, who then retrieved it from the floor and placed it on top of a high pile of signed documents on the edge of the desk.

"Finally finished the paperwork for the week," moaned the Colonel as there was a firm knock on the office door. "Enter," he yelled.

The Baron strode into the office confidently and saluted the Colonel crisply. The salute was completely missed as the Colonel remained pre-occupied with the assisting soldier, balancing the pile of papers whilst walking back to the door.

"Get these off to St. Petersburg," grumbled the Colonel, ignoring the Baron for the moment. "And if any more files come today, lose them or burn them. I have had it with all this paperwork."

The soldier with the paperwork scurried out of the room, closing the door. The Colonel then reached over to an open packet of cigarettes and lit up - allowing time for the exhaled smoke to create a thin veil between himself and the Baron.

"So Baron, you finally decided to grace us with your presence," grinned the Colonel.

The Baron pulled out from his pocket a folded set of papers and stepped forward, placing the papers in front of the Colonel. The Colonel groaned as he balanced his cigarette on the side of an ash tray and unfolded the papers.

"What is this?"

"I am requesting an immediate transfer as a Military Attache to the Russian Delegation at Urga in Outer Mongolia," replied the Baron.

For a moment the Colonel did not look up, as he continued to scan the documents to the very end. Only then, did his facial expression relax as he reached over and recovered his cigarette.

"Are we now?" smiled the Colonel condescendingly. "Why not to the Royal Household, while you are at it?"

"All the paperwork is correct."

Chapter 2

"I have seen that already. That is not the issue."

The Colonel rocked back in his chair and raised his boots onto the side of the desk, while he continued to smoke his cigarette.

"You see Baron, it is not up to me. Your request will have to be processed by the Imperial Foreign Office which could take months or even years. So you are stuck here with me, whether you like it or not."

The Colonel removed his boots from the desk and stubbed out his cigarette, before standing up and walking to the window, to stare outside.

"Anyway, in the end it is the Diplomats who have the final say on the officers attached to their delegations."

The Colonel returned to looking outside, as the Baron stepped forward once more, producing a second document, and reached forward to place it on the desk of the Colonel. Colonel Kukharenko spun around just in time to see the Baron withdrawing his hand and standing back to attention, with the second envelope placed on the desk.

"Oh, you mean this Colonel?" said the Baron in reply.

The face of the Colonel dropped as he moved to sit back down, grabbing a paper knife and slicing open the diplomatic looking envelope to hastily read its contents. Moments later the Colonel dropped his head into his hands.

"Thank you sir," added the Baron. "Good luck sir."

The Colonel didn't look up, but waved with one hand as the Baron saluted, turned and left.

******

Blagoveshchensk Station

At the station, the Baron handed the reins of his horse to a porter, before turning around to Semyonov, Rezukhin and several other Cossack soldiers standing nearby.

"I will miss you comrade," smiled Semyonov. "We could have won a lot of money at cards together."

The Baron bid farewell to Rezukhin and the other soldiers before he smiled and gripped the arms of Semyonov and the two men set off walking to the first class carriages at the other end of the train.

"We will meet again Grigory Mikhaylovich," said the Baron. "But now I have to do this."

Semyonov nodded as the men stop at the door to the first class carriages. "Till then, Baron."

Chapter 2

Semyonov and the Baron hugged, before the Baron stepped onto the train and out of view.

****

Caravan, Road To Urga, Outer Mongolia

Against the sparse backdrop of sub-alpine grasslands and violently hewn mountains, was a caravan of assorted traders and pilgrims on horseback, travelling in single file, along a well worn dusty track. Compared to the immensity of the landscape, the procession seemed insignificant until a closer inspection revealed one of the riders was the Baron.

Further along, the Baron and the caravan passed an old Buddhist Temple attended by pilgrims and marking the entrance into the valley and the city of Urga below them.

****

Urga, Mongolia

The Baron

The ancient city of Urga - full of bright colours, crumbling buildings and medieval living conditions. On the outskirts of a city without sanitation, electricity or running water, the Baron and the caravan pass a desolate stretch of ground where dozens of vultures feast on unrecognisable meat and bones piled onto low stone platforms. Further along at a river nearer at the edge of the city, women and children bathe and clean clothes next to people relieving themselves into the same river.

Within the city, children chased briefly alongside the horse of the Baron, holding out their hands, before the Baron nudged the horse into a faster trot, leaving them behind.

****

Russian Consulate, Urga

The Baron pulled his horse up in front of a two storey building draped in a large Imperial Russian flag, guarded by two Cossacks. The guards on seeing the uniform of the Baron saluted him as he handed the reins of his horse to one of the guards and stepped into the building.

Inside the building, the contrast to the street view was stark. The interior of the consulate resembled more of a wealthy home from St. Petersburg, with polished tiles, and clean painted walls, than a building in a far away outpost. A giant original portrait of the Tsar hung prominently above the main stair case.

As the Baron admired the picture, a junior officer (Borislav Belov) stepped forward into the reception area and saluted him.

"Welcome sir, I am Borislav Anton Belov," said the officer, "head guard of the Consulate."

The Baron looked down at his dirty hands and dust covered uniform and started to brush himself off, before extending his hand to Borislav Belov. At that moment, an officious looking man (Minei Gubelman) stepped forward into the reception area and frowned as a cloud of dust erupted from the uniform of the Baron.

"I am Minei Gubelman," he snapped. "Chief of Staff to the Imperial Russian Consul."

The Baron extended his hand to Minei Gubelman, who promptly ignored it and turned around and started walking away, pointing to an exit in the other direction.

The Baron

"The Soldier's Quarters are that way," he yelled.

Minei Gubelman stopped briefly and turned to look at the Baron.

"You might want to clean up before you meet the Consul."

The Baron nodded and before he could say a word, Minei Gubelman had already turned and walked away.

****

Dressed in a pristine clean white officers uniform of the Russian Imperial Army, the Baron cut a handsome figure, as he stood with Minei Gubelman in front of a set of double doors. Before they opened the doors, Minei Gubelman looked over at the Baron, inspecting his appearance like an overbearing headmistress. He reached over and adjusted the collar of the Baron.

"Better. You might just last the week after all."

Minei Gubelman knocked firmly before entering, with the Baron following him in.

Inside, the spacious private office of the Consul, Alexandre Miller was already up from his desk to greet the Baron before they had even fully arrived in the room. The Baron saluted just as Alexandre Miller extended his hand to greet him.

Chapter 2

"No need for such formalities between ourselves Baron," smiled Alexandre Miller.

Minei Gubelman quickly gave Alexandre Miller a surprised stare, that was acknowledged by Miller as he continued to shake the hand of the Baron.

"Thank you Minei," said Miller waving at Gubelman to leave.

Yet Minei Gubelman remained frozen with a look of surprise and passive disgust. Alexandre Miller now focused his stare at him.

"Minei," he said firmly, "you can leave us, now."

Minei Gubelman hesitated for one more moment as he watched Alexandre Miller ignore him and usher the Baron to a seat opposite his private desk. Minei then let out a passive huff, before he retreated, thumping closed the double doors.

Alexandre Miller stepped over to a side cabinet and selected two glasses, pouring some alcohol from a fine looking crystal decanter.

"Don't worry about Minei," he smiled. "He is officious and pretentious, but ultimately harmless."

Alexandre Miller turned around and handed one of the glasses to the Baron before they raised their glasses. "To Russia!"

"To Russia!" responded the Baron.

"May she survive the growing madness," added Alexandre Miller.

Alexandre Miller reached over with a packet of cigarettes. The Baron declined as he continued to sip his drink, watching as Alexandre Miller lit up a cigarette himself.

"Mongolia is like a rough uncut jewel, cast between ancient mountain gods," said Alexandre Miller in-between sipping his drink and taking puffs of his cigarette. "So long as our mother Russia is crippled by political intrigue and coming war, we do not have the will to seize it for ourselves. Yet the Chinese brood over Mongolia every single moment."

"Yet you saw the Prime Minister hates me," replied the Baron.

Alexandre Miller smiled. "Namnansuren Khan."

"Yes Namnansuren the Khan of -"

"Sain Noyon. Don't worry. That is not such a bad thing."

"You see the real power in Mongolia is with the Bogd Khan who is the third most powerful Buddhist leader behind the Dalai and Panchen Lamas."

Alexandre Miller stood up and grabbed the decanter of alcohol and topped up their glasses. "War is coming Baron. I need someone with enough courage and tenacity. We will be meeting the Bogd Khan in audience this afternoon."

"What is he like?" asked the Baron, causing Alexandre Miller to laugh.

"Don't ask me. In all my time here, I have never had the privilege of speaking with him directly. Few of us mortals ever have."

Alexandre Miller butted out his cigarette. "No. It is more about attending a ritual courtesy of the court. We go in and they announce we are there and we bow and that is that."

"Will the Prime Minister Namnansuren be there?"

"Most probably," grinned Alexandre Miller. "His Holiness the Bogd Khan will be there too, watching everything. But it will be his officials who will speak. His Holiness has a bell. If he is not happy with something, then he is supposed to ring it. But I must confess I have never seen him use it, nor ever speak."

"What do you want me to say then?"

Alexandre Miller smiled again. "Just be yourself," he replied. "They say the Bogd Khan can see into the hearts and souls of men. Who knows, he might even take an interest in yours."

The Baron

Chapter 3

Bogd Khan Palace, Urga

Alexandre Miller and the Baron, accompanied by Borislav Belov and three guards, approached a building resembling at first a vast crumbling ancient Buddhist temple ruin, with countless cracks, broken columns and missing roof tiles. Yet as they stepped closer, its continuous use and importance became clear by the unmistakable presence of guards in traditional Mongolian dress on its steps, while monks moved in and out.

Leaving Borislav Belov and the consulate guards at the footsteps to the palace, the Baron and Alexandre Miller stepped up and into the building and entered into a hallway. There, standing and waiting was Mijiddorjiyn Handdorj and two guards.

"Consul," said Handdorj as be bowed respectfully.

"Foreign Minister," replied Alexandre Miller, also bowing in respect, followed by the Baron, observing the interplay.

Alexandre Miller pointed to the Baron. "Foreign Minister Handdorj let me introduce my new Military Attache Baron von Ungern-Sternberg."

The Baron

Handdorj frowned, without extending any courtesy. "Yes I have heard of you," he said coldly. "Please follow me."

Handdorj and his guard turned around and Alexandre Miller and the Baron followed behind.

****

Alexandre Miller and the Baron followed Handdorj into a great hall full of activity. At the very front, on a raised platform was sitting the Bogd Khan, while Namnansuren was seated in front and to the side of the platform, surrounded by officials. Two dozen support columns, divided the hall into a main thoroughfare through the centre, with the other sides of the columns acting as meeting spaces.

As they shuffled forward, the Baron spotted the British Major Edmund Ironside in conversation with some court officials near a column and he briefly made eye contact with the Baron.

Near the second to last set of columns, Handdorj stopped before four guards, marking a void space between the Bogd Khan and his attendants, before Handdorj signalled to the Court Announcer, who then cried out.

The Baron

"The Imperial Russian Diplomatic Agent and Consul, Alexandre Miller and his Military Attache, requesting an audience with his holiness the Bogd Khan."

Alexandre Miller and the Baron were ushered forward and stopped in front of the Bogd Khan, where Alexandre Miller bowed and the Baron followed suit. Namnansuren appeared preoccupied too with a bundle of documents and did not look up.

"Your Holiness," said Alexandre Miller, "may I present my new Military Attache Baron Roman Nikolai Maximilian von Ungern-Sternberg."

With that, Namnansuren popped his head up like a Meerkat at the announcement and locked eyes with the Baron. Within a short moment, Namnansuren started to turn bright red with anger.

"What is the meaning of this outrage?" he yelled. "Why have you brought this man here?"

Namnansuren signalled to the guards. "Escort the Russian Consul and this man out of the palace. His Holiness is unable to receive him at this time."

Six guards surrounded Alexandre Miller and the Baron indicating them to leave. They turn and start walking back towards the exit to the great hall.

"Stop!"

Chapter 3

The guards and everyone in the court freezed on the spot as nothing but silence could be heard at that moment. The Baron turned around to see the source of the voice, to see the Bogd Khan waving his arm at Namnansuren.

"Am I not the Jebtsundamba?" said the Bogd Khan.

"My Venerable Lord, you are, replied Namnansuren, sounding nervous and in shock at the intervention. "Yet this man is not worthy to be in your presence and is without respect."

"That may be true. But is that not for me to judge my Prime Minister?"

Namnansuren bowed deeply and then sheepishly waved his hands at the guards to return Alexandre Miller and the Baron to the presence of the Bogd Khan.

As they begin to walk back, the Bogd Khan started to climb down from his platform, assisted by two monks. By the time Alexandre Miller and the Baron reached the foot of the platform, the Bogd Khan, a slightly built young man, was standing in front of them both smiling warmly. The Baron looked over at Alexandre Miller who shrugged his shoulders at him in a state of unbelief.

"I have decided that I shall speak with our guest privately," said the Bogd Khan, signalling for the Baron to step forward. "If he is as you say, then he shall no more be welcomed in our lands. But if he is more, then let him reveal his heart and mind."

Namnansuren and the rest of attendants bowed again deeply, as the Bogd Khan started walking and signalled for the Baron to accompany him. As they departed the hall, a series of guards rushed forward and behind, along with attendant monks, leaving Alexandre Miller still standing in the great hall alone.

****

The Bogd Khan and the Baron walked along a long dimly lit corridor, as the few dozen monks they encountered bowed deeply until they passed by.

"You are clearly an educated man, who understands other languages. I hope you do not judge our people on the pride of one, or the mystery of another," said the Bogd Khan.

The Baron bowed respectfully. "I have never met a holy man," he replied.

The Bogd Khan stopped at a set of doors opening up into a lush looking garden. He gestured for the Baron to enter first.

"That makes two of us," responded the Bogd Khan.

Chapter 3

The Bogd Khan and the Baron entered the indoor gardens of beautiful plants and flowing ornamental ponds. After walking a short distance along a pathway between the plants, the Bogd Khan indicated for the Baron to sit with him on a long wooden bench in front of a large ornamental pond.

"It is beautiful here," smiled the Baron.

"But an illusion," replied the Bogd Khan. "A dream of what might be. Our country could be like this paradise, given time. Yet it may also fall victim to the troubles that plagues the rest of the world."

"Our Consul said you are a psychic."

The Bogd Khan started to laugh. "And my Prime Minister fears you will seize and corrupt his only daughter," he chuckled. "It seems we are not so different after all as we both suffer the misunderstandings of others."

The Bogd Khan momentarily stopped laughing and stared at the Baron who seemed uneasy at the power behind the gaze, shifting himself a bit further away on the bench.

"If we settle our minds, then any man or woman reveals themselves by what they say or do not say and what they do or do not. Yet the deeper question is why?"

The Baron

"Why?" replied the Baron shaking his head. "Is that what you are asking me?"

The Bogd Khan remained silent as the Baron continued.

"Why am I here? Why did I join the army? Why do I want to see Erdene?"

"Only you know the answer," said the Bogd Khan, "because only you know the true question."

Now the Baron looked distressed. "I do not know exactly what you mean," he said. "I have literally thousands of questions in my head that start with why?"

"Do not be troubled. This is very good," smiled Bogd Khan. "Many people are so consumed by the superficialities within their lives that they do not give their heart time to even ask. They fill every moment with an obsession of clinging to impermanence, consuming dissatisfaction and wanting more. I can see you on the other hand do not suffer such blindness. Instead you just need a place to start. For example, why did a young man of noble name choose to leave your home?"

"I do not really have a home to speak of," said the Baron. "I grew up in Austria until my parents divorced when I was six and then moved to Estonia with my mother and stepfather. Yet even then, we lived in different cities and cultures around the world. But the place that felt closest to my heart until now is St. Petersburg."

The Bogd Khan clapped his hands. "Wonderful. See, you have answered your own question with your own heart," he beamed. "The only question left is why?"

The Baron scratched his head. "Why St. Petersburg?" he asked. "Is that what you are asking me? Or why am I here?"

A moment of silence passed and then the Bogd Khan abruptly stood up.

"Good," he smiled. "And when you are ready, I will send for you and you can tell me."

The Baron nodded and then followed the Bogd Khan out of the garden.

****

Night-time in Urga - a city without electricity. The Baron was escorted back along the road to the Russian Consulate by two Mongolian Palace guards, holding lanterns on poles. The light of the lanterns flickering off the walls of buildings, exaggerating every shadow, so that even a feral cat cast a shadow like a lion. At the Russian Consulate, the Baron saluted a solitary guard before opening the door.

Inside the consulate, the Baron was shocked and surprised to find a smiling Alexandre Miller and a grumpy Minei Gubelman waiting in the entrance hall for his return.

"All went well with your private meeting, I trust?" asked Alexandre Miller.

"He wants to meet again," replied the Baron. "But didn't say when."

"He missed the opportunity," grumbled Minei Gubelman, trying his best to look disinterested.

Alexandre Miller swung his head around and frowned at Minei Gubelman who stepped back and scampered away.

"In good time," smiled Alexandre Miller. "Nonetheless a major step forward."

Alexandre Miller then moved over to a set of doors separating the entrance area from the reception rooms and opened the door. He stopped and turned to the Baron.

"For now, there is someone who wishes to speak with you."

Chapter 3

Alexandre Miller stepped back allowing the Baron to enter into the reception room alone. Inside the reception room was Erdene in a simple dress, waiting standing with an expectant look, before she smiled broadly at the Baron as he entered.

The Baron quickly looked around the room to see if there was anyone else he has missed.

"It is just me, I came alone," she said.

Alexandre Miller closed the doors to the Reception Room, leaving Erdene and the Baron finally alone.

Erdene produced a white folded fabric square in her hands and walked up to the Baron and bowed. The Baron bowed in return and Erdene in one movement unfolded the square to reveal a long white traditional Buddhist scarf. As the Baron continued to bow, she placed it around his neck and then stepped back.

The Baron straightened up and felt the fabric with his hand.

"It is called a khata," said Erdene. "In Buddhist tradition, it is a gift of good intentions and life."

"Thank you," the Baron smiled warmly. "It is beautiful."

"It is customary to give some positive gift in our culture. I also wanted to ask for your forgiveness for my father."

The Baron

The Baron laughed. "Your father is just trying to protect the honour of his beautiful daughter."

The Baron moved closer, lent down and reached forward, taking the right hand of Erdene and kissed it gently.

"This is a sign of respect and affection in our culture," he said as Erdene started to blush as the Baron stepped back. "In all my life and in all that I have seen," he continued, "I have never encountered someone who encapsulates the extraordinary beauty of this world. It is why I had to see you again."

"My father will be away on business seeing the Chinese General Xu Shuzheng in two days," she replied. "If you wish I can meet you then outside the city walls and then travel to the Duma in the mountains overlooking the whole valley."

The Baron nodded affirmatively. "I would be honoured Princess," he said, causing Erdene to laugh.

"Erdene. You can call me Erdene."

"Very well Erdene, I accept your invitation."

The Baron moved closer again to Erdene, gently placing his right hand on her left shoulder. But as he inched closer, she hesitated and broke free, turning and rushing to the door, before looking back at him.

Chapter 3

"I must go," she said nervously. "There are eyes everywhere. In two days then?"

"Yes, in two days," replied the Baron, bowing once more to her.

Erdene smiled as she opened the door, bowed and then left, leaving the Baron standing alone.

****

On a perfect spring morning, a Mongolian stable hand finishes brushing down a beautiful black horse, with an ornate saddle, before unfastening the reins and escorting it out of the stables.

Standing in the courtyard was Erdene, with Damdini Sukhbaatar and several guards already on their horses. The stable hand brings a black horse to Erdene where she accepts the reins, before the stable hand places a step to the side of the horse and Erdene steps up and onto its back.

****

The Baron was standing in front of a basin and a mirror, preparing and checking and double checking his Imperial Russian Army uniform, when Minei Gubelman came barging in smirking.

"Your rendezvous will have to wait," he beamed. "The Consul wants to see you."

Minei Gubelman turned around and left, as the Baron finished preparing his uniform and followed him.

When the Baron entered the office of the Consul, Alexandre Miller was reading a clutch of papers intently, while smoking a cigarette. As soon as he saw the Baron, he stubbed it out and reached over to his desk and grabbed an envelope, a small box and a satchel, then stood up to greet him.

"You sent for me?" asked the Baron.

"I know you have a little field trip arranged today," replied Alexandre Miller as he handed the Baron the envelope first.

"What is this?" he asked, while opening the letter and reading its contents.

"The Bogd Khan wants to see you this morning. You are expected to attend as soon as we are finished."

The Baron continued to finish reading the letter, while Alexandre Miller opened the small box and produced a silver cross medal, with gold and black ribbon. The Baron looked up as Alexandre Miller came over and started to pin it on his chest.

"Congratulations," smiled Alexandre Miller as he finished pinning the medal on the Baron. "You have been awarded the Cross of Saint George First Class for heroic and undaunted courage at Port Arthur."

The Baron straightened up, as he observed the reflection of the medal in a side mirror in the office, while Alexandre Miller opened the satchel to reveal gold trimming and epaulettes of an Imperial Captain of the Russian Army.

"I also congratulate you on being promoted to Captain of the Imperial Russian Army," added Alexandre Miller as he handed gold trimming and epaulettes to the Baron.

Alexandre Miller walked to his side bar and poured two glasses, while he watched the Baron start adjusting his uniform to put on the epaulettes. He then stepped across, placing the glasses on the edge of the desk, before helping the Baron to adjust the epaulettes.

"Immediately after your meeting with the Bogd Khan we will be leaving for St. Petersburg for a crucial conference," said Alexandre Miller. "In St. Petersburg, we will be discussing with the Chinese and Mongolian delegations a potential treaty concerning Outer

Mongolia. You will be in charge of security as my military attaché."

"I understand," he said as Alexandre Miller handed him a glass.

"Make no mistake Captain," added Alexandre Miller. "This conference is vital for mother Russia to secure her southern and eastern borders, so I am counting on you."

Alexandre Miller raised his glass, followed by the Baron. "To Russia!" cried Alexandre Miller.

"To Russia!" responded the Baron as they finished their toast.

****

The Baron was escorted by Mongolian guards along the hallway he had previously walked with the Bogd Khan to the doorway into the indoor gardens. The guards stop outside and signal for the Baron to step in.

Inside, the beautiful indoor gardens, the Baron retraced the previous path he took to find the Bogd Khan sitting and smiling on the same seat they sat and spoke previously. He signalled for the Baron to sit beside him.

Chapter 3

"You look taller in your new uniform and medals," smiled the Bogd Khan as the Baron sat down next to him. "The Universe never moves in straight lines. I am sorry about the interruption to your journey with Erdene."

The Baron looked at him strangely, before the Bogd Khan laughed. "Remember, I am no psychic. Yet there is little that happens in this kingdom that I am not aware of, especially the movements of my closest advisers and their family," he smiled gently. "You will meet soon enough. Yet, this is not why I have called you."

The Bogd Khan stood up and moved over to a flowering plant and picked a beautiful flower, before returning to the bench. Yet when he returned, the Bogd Khan appeared sombre.

"A terrible War is coming," he said. "You know this. And our people will not be immune from it. Which brings me back to your question?"

"Why?" replied the Baron.

The Bogd Khan smiled briefly, before his face changed to a stern insistence. "No man is asked to do more than he is able. Nor for you as a soldier to question your orders. All I ask is that you consider this question and hold our people in your heart and promise to speak with me on your return."

"Yes, I promise," said the Baron looking confused. "But I do not understand?"

A broad smile returned to the face of the Bogd Khan as he reached into his robes and produced a set of prayer beads, placing them in the hands of the Baron.

"A small gift for your journey," said the Bogd Khan, as the Baron looked at the beads. "We monks use these beads to help us focus, to meditate and to pray. Maybe they will also help you."

The Bogd Khan got up from the bench and patted the Baron on the back, before turning toward the exit. He stopped after a few steps to look at the Baron still sitting fixated on the prayer beads.

"Your Russian Consul is waiting for you," the Bogd Khan said gently.

The Baron picked himself up from the bench and bowed to the Bogd Khan, who bowed in return and both men left the gardens.

****

Chapter 3

High above the city of Urga, on the stone steps of an ancient temple, Erdene sat sadly alone, looking down. She watched in the distance as a troop of riders in Russian uniforms, carrying the Russian flag, galloped out of the city along the road to Irkutsk.

Chapter 4

Irkutsk Train Station

A train flying an Imperial Russian flag and a Mongolian flag, pulled into a platform at Irkutsk Station.

On the platform, was the Baron with some Cossack soldiers. When Rezukhin and Veselovskii got off the recently arrived train, they approached and then saluted the Baron before embracing him.

"A Captain now!" exclaimed Rezukhin.

"Where is Grigory Mikhaylovich?" asked the Baron.

"He has already joined with a new unit under General Aleksey Brusilov," replied Veselovskii. "Near the border of Galicia and the Carpathian Mountains."

"He wants to be a war hero," grinned Rezukhin.

The soldiers watched as Prime Minister Namnansuren and his entourage got onto the train.

"How was Mongolia?" asked Rezukhin.

The Baron ignored him at first as he continued to watch the entourage, including the arrival of the American Captain Elmore Taggart and British Major Edmund Ironside.

The Baron

"A mystery I am yet to fully resolve," he eventually replied, before getting on the train himself.

****

The same train with the Mongolian and Russian flags, continued on its journey to St. Petersburg as night fell.

Inside the Cossack carriage, Elmore Taggart, Edmund Ironside, the Baron and Alexandre Miller were playing cards. In front of Alexandre Miller was a large pile of gold coins, while the other three appear almost broke.

"For a first timer Alexandre, you sure know how to play," groaned Elmore Taggart. The Baron and Edmund Ironside looked equally disheartened.

"You do know that we are stuck on this bloody train for another bloody day and half Miller," grumbled Edmund Ironside. "And at this rate, I might have to take up knitting or singing to pass the time."

Alexandre Miller frowned. "For all these diplomatic journeys, and for the longest time you pleaded with me to play cards and now you don't want me to, on account of me winning? What do you expect me to do then?"

Chapter 4

"How about spreading some charity Alexandre, so we can make a game of it," added Elmore Taggart. "You should certainly be feeling generous after your protégé did so well with the Bogd Khan."

"Yes, yes, you are right," replied Alexandre Miller smiling like a proud parent. He handed ten coins each to Edmund Ironside, Elmore Taggart and the Baron. "Quite extraordinary," he added.

Elmore Taggart nodded in agreement. "After my last report to my shareholders-"

"You mean Washington," interrupted Edmund Ironside.

"Whatever Edmund. They even asked me if you were recruitable?"

"Not before His Majesties Foreign Office has a go of it first. You Americans are always so pushy," responded Edmund Ironside.

"Gentlemen. I am sorry but he is a true patriot and son of Russia," smiled Alexandre Miller.

"Well then Baron, after all the questions we have asked, you still won't tell us what secrets of the universe you discussed?" complained Edmund Ironside. "Alexandre, can't you force him to tell us something?"

General laughter around the table.

"There is nothing to tell," responded the Baron. "He simply asked me about my history and why I joined the army and that I remember the Mongolian people in my prayers."

"But he wanted to meet you twice," responded Elmore Taggart, "and he gave you his prayer beads!"

"Can we see them again Baron?" asked Edmund Ironside, as the Baron nodded and pulled out the prayer beads and handed them to Edmund Ironside, who handled them reverently, before passing them to Alexandre Miller who also studied them carefully.

"In all my time in Mongolia, I have not even said boo to his holiness the Bogd Khan," added Edmund Ironside, "and you are there five minutes and suddenly you are best friends."

Elmore Taggart slapped the Baron on the back, as he received the prayer beads back from Alexandre Miller.

"You are an enigma Baron that is for sure," grinned Elmore Taggart.

****

St. Petersburg

Chapter 4

A bleak and wet morning in St. Petersburg. The Baron and guards accompanied Alexandre Miller and Minei Gubelman across the vast Hermitage Palace Square. They stopped at the main gate of the unmistakable wedding-cake edifice of the Winter Palace.

At the entrance, Alexandre Miller turned to the Baron. "The Chinese delegation will be here shortly, followed by the Mongolians, who want to be the last to arrive," he said. "You of course are welcome to accompany me and get out of this weather. But the men are not permitted within the palace."

The Baron smiled. "I am fine. I will stay with the men."

Alexandre Miller shrugged his shoulders, turned and walked through the palace gates, with Minei Gubelman smirking behind.

"Can I take your place Captain, if you don't want to stay dry?" asked Veselovskii, to a round of laughter among the Cossacks.

The Baron shook his head at Veselovskii. "You know as well as I Stepan Borisovich that if I did accompany the Consul, I would be the laughing stock of all Cossacks from here to the Carpathians."

More laughter among the troops as they eyeball the arrival of the Chinese delegation to the main gate of the

The Baron

Winter Palace, led by Xu Shuzheng. A few moments later, the Baron and his Cossack troops watch as Prime Minister Namnansuren and the Mongolian Delegation arrived at the gates. Namnansuren and the Baron briefly lock eyes for a second, with Namnansuren allowing himself a brief smirk, similar to Minei Gubelman, at the sight of the Baron standing in the rain.

Not long after, Elmore Taggart and Edmund Ironside arrived. Before they were about to enter, Elmore Taggart spotted the Baron standing in the rain with the other soldiers.

"Baron, for goodness sake," grinned Elmore Taggart as he stepped closer along with Edmund Ironside, "you'll die of hypothermia."

"It is nothing," replied the Baron, as Elmore Taggart looked at the entrance gates and then back at Edmund Ironside, before shrugging his shoulders.

"Edmund, you go in and let me know. I have seen enough diplomatic meetings," smiled Elmore Taggart. "Come with me Baron and I'll show you the real heart of St. Petersburg."

"Suit yourself," replied Edmund Ironside. "But if they start dividing up mineral rights, I might be forced to rethink our alliance."

Chapter 4

Elmore Taggart laughed as Rezukhin looked at the Baron and shook his head negatively.

"It's only a Coffee Shop two hundred metres across from the square on Nevsky Avenue next to the Moyka embankment," added Elmore Taggart. "If it makes you feel better we can sit near the front windows with the Anarchists. Or you can still see the palace from the back tables with the Bolsheviks."

The Baron looked back at Rezukhin. "Come and get me if they leave early. I won't be long," he said.

Rezukhin nodded as Elmore Taggart slapped the back of the Baron.

"Excellent! One coffee or tea, on me. I will even show you the seat where Pushkin had his last drink before his fateful duel in 1837."

****

Elmore Taggart sipped a coffee and the Baron a tea, at a table at the front of the The Literary Cafe. Other patrons looked on wearily.

"You are a strange fish Baron," smiled Elmore Taggart as the Baron frowned and glanced over at the various faces of the other coffee shop patrons. "On the one hand," continued Elmore Taggart, "you are smart enough to be beyond all this and yet you choose to wear the uniform and follow the orders of madmen."

"I am but a soldier," replied the Baron.

Taggart laughed. "Look around Baron," said Elmore Taggart as he gestured with a grand sweep of his arm. "Here in this tiny coffee shop are some of the future leaders of Russia."

Taggart signalled the Baron to look at a table at the back of the cafe.

"Do you see that table up there? Now do you see that distinguished looking man everyone is huddled around? We'll that's Alexei Rykov, just returned from Paris and the real brain behind the Bolsheviks. Not Lenin or Trotsky. Actually the fellow with the glasses and moustache next to him is Lev Kamenev is the brother-in-law to Leon Trotsky."

"So why don't the Secret Police arrest them?"

"They already have more than once in the past and probably will again soon. But you see the fact is that the people of Russia have had enough of the corruption of the aristocracy. No offence."

"None taken."

"I fully understand the attraction of the romantic and noble notion of fighting and dying for your adopted homeland," said Elmore Taggart. "But trust me when I say, the future of the new world is to be found in coffee shops like these in major cities, not in the killing fields of battle."

"Yes, you are not the first to share this perspective," replied the Baron. "Yet, what is any man if he denies his own soul?"

Elmore Taggart shook his head. "That's the thing. I am not trying to change you. It is just you could do so much more," he smiled. "You could truly be a powerful figure in the future of this country."

"Are you trying to recruit me captain?" smiled the Baron.

The Baron looked back outside to see the figure of Rezukhin running down the street toward the cafe.

"No, not in so many words," replied Elmore Taggart, "But the question is Baron, will you - "

The Baron put his hand up as he jumped up out of his seat.

"Thank you for the coffee," smiled the Baron. "But I must go."

He stepped outside to greet Rezukhin slightly short of breath.

"They have finished early," said Rezukhin. "Something about the Chinese not being happy with the equal seating arrangement around the table."

The Baron

Rezukhin and the Baron hurried back to the Palace Square where Alexandre Miller and Minei Gubelman were waiting.

"I heard Elmore Taggart led you astray to one of my favourite places," said Alexandre Miller. "I hope he wasn't trying to recruit you."

"I am sorry," replied the Baron. "It won't happen again."

"If I was in charge, I would have you shot for desertion," muttered Minei Gubelman, causing Alexandre Miller to scowl at him.

"That is why, thank God you, Minei, will never be in charge of any court or high office," responded Alexandre Miller. "At least not in my lifetime."

Minei Gubelman huffed off on his own, leaving Alexandre Miller and the Baron.

"Ignore Minei Gubelman," said Alexandre Miller. "While he is an excellent secretary, he is a horrible judge of character and remains jealous of the world."

"Yet it is true. I am a soldier and this is my post," added the Baron.

"Nonsense. I did not want you to wait out here in the rain, nor are you compelled to stand in this square for hours. No, tomorrow morning after we arrive, I insist you go and enjoy a coffee at the Literary Cafe, without being disturbed," smiled Alexandre Miller.

****

A bright blue morning in St. Petersburg. The Baron was sitting alone at a table close to the front windows of the The Literary Cafe, lost in his own thoughts and the passing world of people.

"Roman Nikolaivich, it would be an honour if we could meet your acquaintance," said a voice from behind the Baron.

He swung around to see Alexei Ivanovich Rykov standing next to the table. Rykov bowed and then smiled as the Baron narrowed his stare at him.

"How do you know me?"

"Oh Baron, you are quite famous among many circles in this city," replied Rykov. "A legend to some and a mystery to others."

"I thought your kind only lived in the darkness and smoke," grinned the Baron. "I did not think the Bolsheviks came this close to sunlight."

Rykov laughed as many sets of eyes within the cafe watched the exchange intently.

The Baron

"For you Baron Roman Nikolai Maximilian von Ungern-Sternberg, I am more than willing to make an exception." Rykov signalled a table at the back of the cafe, that Elmore Taggart had pointed out the day earlier. "Please, would you join us, even for the briefest moment? You have nothing to fear. It might even add to the mystery that is the Baron."

The Baron followed Rykov to the table, where Rykov pointed to Lev Borisovich Kamenev.

"Baron, this is Lev Borisovich Kamenev," said Rykov as Kamenev extended his hand.

"I know who you are and about your brother in law," replied the Baron. "Why do you wish to speak with me?"

"Surely, you must know that many speak of you just as many also speak of the mystic Grigori Yefimovich," said Kamenev.

"Rasputin," added the Baron.

"A man borne to title, to wealth, who throws all of it away to be with the people. Who shows his courage in battle and even now pursues his heart," said Kamenev. "For such a story to be real, is a paper editors dream!"

"Is that what my life is to you? A means of selling more editions of Pravda," growled the Baron. "You are bank robbers and propagandists. I have nothing in common with the Bolsheviks."

"That is where you are wrong my friend," smiled Rykov. "It is true we were not borne into privilege like you. But we know what it is like to go to war, to fight for something you believe in. Soon this world of Imperial Russia will end and the people will look to new heroes. We are their voice and writers of these new stories."

The Baron got up from his chair. "You people know nothing of the horror of war, nor of the benefit of the people," he said. "All you crave is power. Nothing more."

"Be warned Baron," said Kamenev. "A fine line exists between the hero and the anti-hero. We can stoke the furnaces of revolution by your story being either a saviour of the people or a villain. The readers will never know or care for the truth. So the choice is ultimately yours."

The Baron turned his head and left.

****

Alexandre Miller and Minei Gubelman stepped out through the gates of the Winter Palace and looked over as the Baron and Rezukhin marched over to meet them.

"We leave for once for Urga," said Alexandre Miller angrily.

The Baron nodded affirmatively.

"You are to personally escort the Prime Minister with your best soldiers and remain with him on the train," added Alexandre Miller. "Do you understand?"

"The outcome?" asked the Baron.

Alexandre Miller shook his head. "Outer Mongolia is lost," he sighed. "The Imperial Court has handed it to the Chinese Government of Duan Qirui."

Alexandre Miller, the Baron and Minei Gubelman continued to walk away from the palace as the Baron looked back to see Prime Minister Namnansuren and the rest of his entourage exit through the palace gates, stony-faced. The Baron looked across at Alexandre Miller.

"Why?" he asked. "It makes no sense."

"Appeasement," replied Alexandre Miller. "They would rather forget about the east and worry about the south and west."

Alexandre Miller stopped walking at the sight of the Mongolian delegation leaving.

Chapter 4

"You have your orders then, said Alexandre Miller. "No contact with any external parties. No Americans, British or French."

The Baron and Rezukhin saluted, then turned and followed behind Prime Minister Namnansuren and the Mongolian Delegation as they walked past the stationary Alexandre Miller and Minei Gubelman.

****

Train to Irkutsk

A train at night barrelled along the seemingly endless tracks of the Trans-Siberian line. The internal lights of the carriages flickered as the train sped past the nightscape.

Inside the official Mongolian carriage, Namnansuren was busily writing at a desk, while Rezukhin was sitting half-asleep on a chair close to the doorway. No other Mongolian guards or officials were in the carriage when the Baron entered. The Baron tapped Rezukhin on the shoulder.

"Get some rest Borisovich. I'll see you in the morning."

The Baron

Rezukhin looked up at first before getting up from the chair. Once he had left the carriage, Namnansuren stopped writing and looked at the Baron.

"You cannot keep my men as prisoners or hold me as hostage. This is an outrage."

"I am only following orders Prime Minister," replied the Baron.

Namnansuren laughed as the Baron moved over to a sofa chair close to the writing desk of the Prime Minister. Namnansuren put down his papers and moved over to the sofa chair opposite the Baron.

"And yet your affections for my daughter would see you travel a thousand miles to a strange land."

The Baron scowled at him. "Do you question my honour to my country?"

Namnansuren smiled. "Whether your head likes it or not, you are now bound to the destiny of Mongolia. If you let me speak to the British, French or Americans?"

"I have my orders Prime Minister. I am not a diplomat."

"Oh but you are Baron. You pretend to be a soldier, but really you know you are more a leader than all of them. Why do you lie to yourself?"

Awkward silence.

Chapter 4

"Surely you cannot believe that what you have done will mean nothing to the Bogd Khan, or my daughter?" added Namnansuren.

The Baron stared at Namnansuren for a moment, before getting up and walking back to the same chair that Rezukhin had been sitting in.

The Baron

Chapter 5

The train pulled into the platform at Irkutsk Station. Standing on the platform with Damdini Sukhbaatar and several Mongolian Guards was Erdene. Moments later, when Namnansuren appeared, Erdene rushed forward and hugged him as the rest of the Mongolian delegation exited the train. Alexandre Miller, Minei Gubelman then the Baron and Rezukhin stepped off the train. The Baron looked over to see Erdene with her father.

At first Erdene did not seem to acknowledge the Baron, while her father was speaking into her ear. Then, without any warning, she scowled at the Baron and launched herself across to where he was standing, brushing past Alexandre Miller and Minei Gubelman. She slapped the Baron hard across the face.

"There was nothing I could do," apologised the Baron, as Erdene wiped her face.

"Everyone has a choice," she replied coldly. "I shall never acknowledge you or speak to you again."

Erdene, then turned on her heels and rushed away to catch up to her father Namnansuren as they were leaving the platform. The Baron watched her depart before turning back to see Alexandre Miller and Minei Gubelman deeply engrossed in a telegram.

The Baron walked over as Alexandre Miller looked up and snatched the telegram from the hands of Minei Gubelman. He then handed the telegram to the Baron, as Gubelman sneered.

"Franz Ferdinand has been assassinated in Sarajevo," said Alexandre Miller.

"It has started then," replied the Baron.

The Baron studied the telegram for a few more moments before looking up at Alexandre Miller and straightened himself up to attention.

"I request immediate release for active duty to the 34th Regiment a Galicia," said the Baron to Alexandre Miller.

Alexandre Miller laughed.

"You can't be serious? It will be a bloodbath!"

Alexandre Miller kept looking at the Baron who did not twitch as Minei Gubelman broke into a smile. Alexandre Miller then started to shake his head negatively as he took back the telegram.

"I know you know that I cannot stop you," said Alexandre Miller. "I also know you know first hand that war can be hell. Yet this war will be something altogether more terrible."

****

Proskurov Galicia

The Baron was now in a picturesque town, full of colour and men in military uniforms. He walked past a group of soldiers standing at the edge of a town square, smoking and making cat calls at girls nearby. The Baron smiled as he passed a cafe and grocer shop in the square with their bright coloured awnings and the grocers display of fresh fruits.

The Baron stopped two soldiers, who saluted, and then gave him directions. They pointed to a different direction outside the square, before saluting again and hurrying away.

****

Eighth Army Headquarters, Proskurov Galacia 1914

On the outskirts of the colourful town, on a perfectly sunny spring day, soldiers were practising drills and riding horses in lines, while a group of officers watched on, under the shade of a white military tent.

As the Baron approached, the guards at the front of the tent saluted. A moment later, the bounding figure of Grigory Mikhaylovich Semyonov came flying out toward the Baron.

"So you've given up on women and decided to join us!" shouted Semyonov, before the two men embraced.

"I couldn't let you steal all the glory Grigory Mikhaylovich," grinned the Baron.

At the shouting outside, the officers within the tent stopped talking and watched as the Baron and Semyonov slapped each other on the back. Semyonov then grabbed the Baron and pushed him into the tent and into the path of Colonel Pyotr Nikolayevich Wrangel.

The Baron stiffly saluted before identifying himself. "Roman Nikolai Maximilian von Ungern-Sternberg."

Wrangel instead extended his hand to the Baron. They shake. "I know who you are," he said.

Wrangel then returned his attention to a large military map on which pieces were placed. He then pointed to a particular part of the map.

"The objective of the Eighth Army of General Brusilov is to capture central Galicia to the Carpathian

Mountains, supported by General Ruzski of the Third Army, while the Fifth Army of General Plehve and Fourth Army of General Salza surrounding the Austrians further north-west."

Wrangel stopped and looked straight at the Baron.

"I know about Port Arthur Captain. But this might be closer to home," said Wrangel. "Will there be any problem with the Austrians?"

The Baron shook his head. "Russia is my mother and my heart Colonel," he replied.

One of the officers (Leonid Sipailov) standing next to Semyonov looked at him strangely, as Wrangel resumed concentrating on the map, pointing to a different spot.

"He was borne in Austria," whispered Semyonov to Sipailov.

"Our primary enemy is General Rudolph von Brudermann of the Austrian third army and a career soldier and formidable opponent," said Wrangel. "The job of the 34th Regiment will be to move ahead of the army and locate precisely the enemy and if necessary engage the enemy."

Semyonov shook his head negatively. "The Austrians have the latest high repetition machine guns don't they sir?"

Wrangel nodded his head affirmatively.

"And we are cavalry," added Semyonov.

"Then use your initiative Captain," snapped Wrangel. "Of course I do not expect you to gallop head long into a wall of machine gun nests. But use your imagination. After all, you now have your comrade the Baron here to help."

****

Urga, Russian Embassy

Sunlight burst through the blinds of a bedroom, while Alexandre Miller remained fast asleep under the covers. There was a knock at the bedroom door before an attendant entered carrying a tray and a pot of tea with a cup.

"Your excellency."

The attendant waited nervously as around the room, the cabinet and light shade and fittings and then the bed start to rumble. Alexandre opened up his eyes and started to stir as the rumbling got louder.

"For goodness sake. No need to be rude," said Alexandre Miller at first disorientated and thinking the attendant was doing something. His face then changed when he soon realised that everything in the room and building was shaking in unison.

Minei Gubelman then bounded into the room brushing past the attendant, who nervously caught the teapot before it was about to fall off the tray.

Alexandre Miller now had both eyes open and was upright in bed as the whole room and building was now violently shaking, before he looked over at Minei Gubelman hovering like a vulture.

"The Chinese have invaded!"

Alexandre Miller jumped out of the bed, grabbing a dressing gown in the process, before opening the door to a balcony. He stepped back for a moment on opening the door at the cloud of dust and noise that filled the room, before stepping onto the balcony.

On the balcony, the Russians observe the Chinese line of horses, trucks and troops passing the stunned and frightened looking inhabitants of the city.

A car carrying General Xu Shuzheng motored past the Russian embassy as the Chinese general looked up at the Russians on the balcony. Xu Shuzheng smiled and gave a faux salute before looking back ahead.

Alexandre Miller looked over at Minei Gubelman.

"Telegraph St. Petersburg. Tell them what is happening. The Chinese have arrived."

The Baron

Minei Gubelman bowed dutifully and scurried away as Alexandre Miller returned to watching the passing parade of Chinese troops.

Chapter 6

Bogd Khan Palace Steps

General Xu Shuzheng was standing on the steps of the Bogd Khan Palace as the Chinese troops behind him finished unfurling long Chinese flags over the front of the palace. A nervous looking Namnansuren Khan, Erdene and Mijiddorjiyn Handdorj were standing behind and to the left of General Xu Shuzheng.

Chinese troops lined the street as a crowd of people gathered to watch, while Alexandre Miller and Minei Gubelman shuffled through the crowd to get a better view.

"People of Urga, you have nothing to fear," said Xu Shuzheng. "See, your leaders are still your leaders. Yet your protector is now China and not Russia."

Xu Shuzheng then turned to Namnansuren. "Wave to the crowd and show we are allies," he said.

"The Mongolian people will never lay down as slaves," whispered Namnansuren. "They will fight and resist you."

The crowd went deathly silent, almost as if they were collectively straining to hear the conversation.

"Then for the sake of their children and your daughter I hope you can persuade them otherwise," replied Xu Shuzheng.

"We are not afraid to die," said Namnansuren.

"I know Prime Minister," said Xu Shuzheng still smiling for the crowd.

Xu Shuzheng then made a sweep with his hand around the steps and the Bogd Khan Palace behind them.

"But if the house falls, so does its shrines and temples," he said. "The safety of the Bogd Khan is assured for now. But I can only assure such safety if the city holds. If it does not -"

Namnansuren stepped forward to be next to Xu Shuzheng. He gave a half-smile as Xu Shuzheng grabbed his hand and raised it to the cheers of the crowd.

****

Prime Minister's House, Urga

Chinese soldiers were standing grimly outside the building. Namnansuren and Erdene were standing in the courtyard, with Damdini Sukhbaatar in the distance, as Erdene prepared the saddle on a horse.

"His holiness will grant you sanctuary," said Namnansuren.

Namnansuren handed Erdene a package of papers.

"But I want to stay with you," protested Erdene.

"It is too dangerous. These papers will get you through," said Namnansuren before Erdene embraced and kissed her father. "Trust no one," he added.

Namnansuren looked over in the direction of Damdini Sukhbaatar and then back at Erdene.

"What will happen to you?" she asked.

"As long as I know you are safe my daughter, then nothing of harm may come to me. Now go, before it is too late."

Erdene gets on her horse and wipes her tears. As Damdini Sukhbaatar came over and Namnansuren waved his hands.

"It is fine Damdini. She is only going on a short errand, so you can keep me company."

Damdini bowed his head and watched as Erdene left the compound, past the Chinese guards.

****

The Baron

Austria-Hungarian Lines

An eerie silence as morning mist still hugged the fields. An Austrian Officer moved from one machine gun nest under the trees to another.

"Stay alert," said the officer.

The Officer stopped behind one machine gun nest as he hears bird noises, then the sound of trumpets across the fields.

"Here they come."

Then in the distance appeared one, then five then fifty then over a hundred horses spread out across the lines, creating a huge cloud of dust.

"There are no riders or saddles," shouted one of the soldiers.

"They are Cossacks and they can hide like ghosts, open fire!" demanded an officer.

The Officer stepped forward. "Commence firing," he yelled.

But none of the Austrian guns started firing as the horses continued to gallop toward the Austrian lines.

"Sir they're just horses, there is no one on them or on the side of them."

Frustrated, the officer moved further out in front and raised his pistol, taking aim at an approaching horse and began firing. Soon after other shots began ringing out, but no machine gun fire. The gun shots only strengthened the chaos of the stampede toward the Austrian lines.

Soon the riderless horses and dust were upon the Austrian lines. The officer continued to fire, shielding his eyes until a panicked horse hit him in full gallop, sending him cartwheeling to the ground. Other soldiers and officers began to abandon their positions, while a few lowered their heads and hid.

"Cease fire. Cease fire," yelled another Austrian officer after the last horse had fled and the dust had subsided. "Advance," he commanded.

The Austrian troops then began to slowly advance from the tree line into the fields in front of their former positions. Moments later, when they were just a few steps in front of the trees, out of the grass popped hundreds of Cossacks, including the Baron and Semyonov. Within seconds of a terrible volley, most of the Austrians are struck down.

Moments later, the Baron and the other Cossacks rushed forward and shoot dead the Austrian soldiers running back to try and secure the machine guns. As fast as the violence had begun, the scene was soon quiet as the gun smoke started to dissipate.

The Baron

Slowly and methodically, the Cossacks check each Austrian soldier, while executing the dying or wounded. A wounded Austrian officer pretended to be dead as the Baron stepped past him. Semyonov walked back from the other way greeted the Baron.

"Great plan Grigory Mikhaylovich," grinned Semyonov.

As if in slow motion, the Baron watched as Semyonov whipped out his service revolver and pointed it at the head of the Baron and pulled back the trigger. Instinctively, the Baron jumped out of the way and onto the ground.

Behind the Baron, the figure of the bloodied Austrian officer crumpled to the ground dead. The Baron picked himself up to see Semyonov smiling.

"Sorry for that."

Semyonov then pulled out a flare gun and fired the flare up into the air. Off in the distance many hundreds of mounted Cossacks began to appear onto the fields.

"Now we have to go and find our horses," said Semyonov.

Chapter 7

Against the backdrop of jagged mountains, Semyonov and a group of other Cossacks including captain Leonid Sipailov were relaxing, drinking coffee and smoking around a fire next to a small stream. They watched as the shirtless Baron, further down the stream, washed clean his khata scarf in the water. The prayer beads dangling from his belt.

"Souvenir Baron?" said Sipailov, pointing to the prayer beads.

The Baron stopped washing, turned and smiled. "A gift," he replied. "It is supposed to bring protection and good luck."

Semyonov started laughing.

"That's funny. Because I thought the last time she saw you, she slapped you so hard, you have the scar to prove it. So not so lucky after all."

Sipailov and the rest of the men started laughing as the figures of Rezukhin and Veselovskii in fresh uniforms appeared. Semyonov was the first to spot them.

"Stepan and Borisovich you have made it!"

Semyonov bounded over and embraced each of the men.

"We couldn't let Grigory Mikhaylovich have all the glory, could we?" said Rezukhin, as the Baron stepped over and embraced them warmly.

More laughter filled the air before the stern figure of Wrangel accompanied by his aide walked up to the officers and men. The Baron saw him first and stood to attention.

"Attention!" yelled the Baron.

Wrangel waved his hand.

"At ease."

"Colonel?" asked Semyonov.

"We've been ordered to pull back," said Wrangel to a wave of collective groaning.

"What? Pull back?" growled Semyonov. "We just smashed the whole third Austro-Hungarian army and the Carpathians and now they want us to withdraw? This is madness - "

"Grigory Mikhaylovich," said the Baron interrupting the ranting of Semyonov.

Semyonov stopped and composed himself.

"General Alexander Samsonov is dead and the 2nd Army has ceased to exist at Tannenberg," added

Wrangel. "So it doesn't matter how far we have advanced into Hungary, if we lose all of Prussia."

Semyonov and the others shook their heads at the news, as Wrangel turned around to leave.

"Tell the men to mount up," said Wrangel. "We move out tonight."

Semyonov and the Baron salute as Wrangel walked away.

"I am telling you Baron," grumbled Semyonov, "we will never be sitting here again in this war. At least not in Russian uniforms."

The Baron smiled as he wrapped the khata around his neck and put on his shirt.

"Remember we were warned Grigory Mikhaylovich," said the Baron. "A bloodbath right?"

Semyonov laughed.

"Yes, a bloodbath."

****

Bogd Khan Palace

In the hallway, the traditional Mongolian guards stood aside as Damdini Sukhbaatar dressed in a smart

Chinese uniform and accompanied by six other Chinese soldiers brushed past.

Inside, the Great Hall was virtually empty except for a handful of people. At one end, the Bogd Khan was reading on his raised platform, while Erdene was burrowing through documents on a table in front. At the sound of stomping boots on the ancient stone floor, she looked up to see the approaching Chinese soldiers accompanying an officer she did not at first recognise.

"What is this outrage," she yelled. "You have no right to be here."

"The Head of Security and Public Order, Captain Damdini Sukhbaatar," replied Damdini Sukhbaatar at the same time Erdene recognised him.

Damdini Sukhbaatar motioned to the soldiers to stay as he moved forward to Erdene.

"You!" she growled at Damdini. "A man my father trusted."

"We each do what we have to, so we survive Princess."

"By betraying your own people?"

A single bell began ringing and echoing throughout the Great Hall and Erdene went silent. Erdene looked up at the Bogd Khan holding the bell and acknowledged his frown, before looking back at a smiling Damdini Sukhbaatar.

"As much as it may surprise you princess," he continued, "I am here on official business of the Chinese Government."

"How can we help you and the Government of China Captain?" she replied deadpan.

"As Head of Security and Public Order, I am responsible for ensuring that peace is maintained," he said in a pompous tone, "and that any people seeking to harm that peace and security are brought to justice."

"We also desire the safety of the people," said the Bogd Khan from his platform.

"Yes your holiness," replied Damdini Sukhbaatar as he looked up. "But it has come to my attention that there may be people who are taking advantage of your good will and hiding fugitives within these walls."

"What do you propose then?" added the Bogd Khan.

"I ask only that you appoint a trusted agent, someone such as ...say... Princess Erdene who will accompany me as we conduct a discrete search of the buildings and vouch that no dissidents are being provided safe harbour."

"No, I will not do it. Not with you -"

The Baron

"Now Erdene," said the Bogd Khan interrupting her. "We all must do things sometimes we would otherwise not do. Sitting on this tower every day for example. The Captain wishes you no harm. Accompany him and show him our hospitality and keep me informed."

Damdini Sukhbaatar gave Erdene a creepy smile, as Erdene bowed her head to the Bogd Khan, before looking up straight at him.

"Very well. But I want your solemn oath here, in this place, that no harm will come to my father and that I may freely visit him."

"You know your father is wilful Princess," said Damdini Sukhbaatar. "How can I then make such a promis-"

"If you do not or cannot or will not," she said interrupting him, "then I cannot accept the role being asked of me."

The Bogd Khan smiled as Damdini Sukhbaatar looked up at him, waiting, hoping for some instruction.

"Very well," sighed Damdini Sukhbaatar

"Very well what?" demanded Erdene.

"I so promise."

Erdene bowed to Damdini Sukhbaatar.

"Then I look forward to accompanying you Captain during your inspection of the palace."

Erdene looked up at the Bogd Khan.

"But for now your holiness, I bid leave to prepare to visit my father under the solemn protection of the Captain."

The Bogd Khan bowed with a beaming smile on his face as Erdene departed.

****

Chinese Prison

A group of Chinese soldiers were sitting on stools in a dimly lit medieval looking room. A prisoner nearby with a mop and bucket was washing away blood from a bench and the floor. The door opened to reveal Erdene, followed by some other guards.

The Chinese soldiers stared at her leeringly, before she defiantly stepped forward and handed one of them a set of papers. He looked at them and then back at Erdene, before grunting, turning and picking up a set of keys hanging on the wall.

"Follow me," one of them barked at her.

The Baron

The guard started walking away down a corridor and Erdene hurried after him. They stop at a grill gate and a set of torches fastened to a rack. The guard reached up and lit a torch, handing it to her, before lighting one for himself and opening the gate.

Erdene and the guard walk down a steep flight of wet stone stairs, illuminated only by the old style flame sticks held by Erdene and the Chinese Guard. He stopped at the bottom of the steps before a door, turning the key in the lock and then stepped back away.

"You have ten minutes."

Erdene at first hesitated, before bowing down and entering through the door.

Erdene entered into the cell, her torch illuminating the grim and dirty walls. The scratched carvings and scrawls of previous condemned captives were highlighted by the flames.

"Father? Father where are you?"

In the corner of the cell, Erdene heard a shuffling sound and quickly turned around, shining the torch in front of her face, to reveal the mere shadow of a once proud man, dirty, broken and bloody. At first Erdene recoiled in fright.

Chapter 7

"Please daughter, move the light away. I do not want you to see me like this."

Erdene ignored his plea and rushed over, embracing his frail and dirty frame, until he too embraced her.

"What have they done to you? What has happened to the house and the servants?"

Namnansuren lets out a weak laugh-cough.

"But alas a memory my beautiful daughter. As soon so shall I be. How then did you come here?"

"Damdini Sukhbaatar."

Namnansuren nodded his head.

"I do not condemn a man doing what he must to survive, even Damdini."

"He is a traitor."

"No. He is a realist as you also must be," said Namnansuren. "No one is coming to save you. The Russian Baron is long gone."

"Good."

Namnansuren let off another cough.

"Do not be so quick to judge my daughter. I regret not telling you this earlier, but the young Baron did truly have deep affection for you. He told me. I saw in his eyes the struggle with his own loyalty to Russia and his affection to you. Yet as much as I tried, I could not persuade him to compromise to my ego."

"Why are you telling me this now?"

"What happened was not his fault. Maybe you should write to him. Maybe he is still alive after all this war."

Erdene started to cry. "I don't want you to die."

Namnansuren reached over and stroked her hair.

"My daughter you of all people should know the answer to that. No-one we truly love ever really dies."

****

Bogd Khan Palace, Erdenes Room

Erdene sat at a desk lit by candle light, writing a letter as Buddhist monks chanted their evening prayers.

Dear Baron.

Erdene scratched out the words and started again.

Dear Roman Nikolai.

****

As Erdine wrote her letter the Baron, Semyonov and the Cossack comrades of Rezukhin, Veselovskii and Sipailov were in fierce hand to hand combat against the Austrian-Hungarian troops. The faces of the fighting men animated with rage and horror as some men kill and other men are brutally killed.

I hope and pray you are still alive. Much has happened since you left Mongolia. The Chinese have taken control and my father is their prisoner.

In the aftermath of the battle the Cossacks pick over the dead and tend to the wounded.

I also hope my gifts have protected you against all this violence in the world.

The Baron washed the blood off his body and the blood out of the white khata.

I wish to apologise as my father told me it was not your fault when you missed our appointment. I am safe under the protection of the Bogd Khan.

I pray this letter reaches you without delay and that you write to me and we meet again soon. Erdene

****

The Baron, Semyonov, Rezukhin, Veselovskii and Sipailov and their soldiers relaxed along the side of a road, as the wounded crawled and shuffled past them.

The Baron

In the distance, midst all the Russian soldiers in uniform, the strange figure of two Buddhist monks in traditional dress appear walking along the side of the road. Semyonov spotted them first and prodded the Baron to sit up and see.

"Look. Look. They've come to take you back comrade!"

The rest of the soldiers laugh as the Baron glanced over and then closed his eyes. There was continued laughter and jeering as the two Buddhist monks shuffled closer and closer until they stop in front of Semyonov and the Baron, standing in serene silence.

The Baron opened his eyes to see the two Buddhist Monks standing in front of him, with their heads bowed. The Baron looked over at Semyonov who shrugged his shoulders.

"Can I help you?" asked the Baron.

"Are you Baron Roman Nikolai Maximilian von Ungern-Sternberg?" one the monks asked quietly.

The Baron nodded and one of the the Buddhist monks handed him a letter, before both monks turned and departed back down the road shuffling past the Russian troops and trucks. The Baron ripped open the envelope and started reading.

Chapter 7

"Well? What does it say?" asked Semyonov expectantly.

"It says don't trust Semyonov with alcohol or secrets," smiled the Baron.

The rest of the men started laughing as the Baron put the letter back in the envelope and carefully into his left breast pocket and smiled.

The Baron

Chapter 8

South-Eastern Front

A grim alien world devoid of any redemption. A stark reminder of the cruelty of men. Torn strips of uniforms snagged upon piles of barbed wire, damaged steel, sand bags and rotting flesh.

Sitting under a makeshift awning out of the rain and the mud, the Baron began penning a letter.

My dearest Erdene, your letter brought me light and beauty in an otherwise awful world.

****

As the Baron wrote his letter, the monotonous slaughter and futility of trench warfare continued. The Baron and other Russian soldiers were called over the trenches into a no-mans land, where men are slaughtered by machine guns and others are suspended in the barbed wire like hellish scarecrows. Yet the Baron survived.

I have seen the worst of men and the best of men.

Midst the horror, Wrangel, the Baron and Semyonov stood in immaculate uniforms as the visiting Tsar Nicholas pinned medals on their chests.

Yet it is the thought that one day I will see you again, that makes each day in this madness worthwhile.

When this war ends and I can leave. I will return and God willing, will do all in my power to help free your father and Mongolia.

****

Urga

A young boy was running with a letter along a dirty street toward the Bogd Khan Palace, before being stopped by Damdini Sukhbaatar.

****

Damdini Sukhbaatar sat at a desk, reading and re-reading the letter.

There was a knock at the door and he put down the letter, before a soldier opened the door and saluted.

Chapter 8

The soldier stepped aside, allowing Erdene to enter the room, looking nervous.

"Ah yes Erdene. Please come in," said Damdini Sukhbaatar before signalling to the soldier, "you can leave us."

The soldier closed the door, leaving Damdini Sukhbaatar and Erdene alone. Erdene scanned the room, noticing a letter, before looking back at Sukhbaatar.

"Have a seat," smiled Damdini Sukhbaatar.

"I'd rather stand."

"Suit yourself," he replied, picking up the letter. "You know, it is not easy for me to do what I have to do to protect the people. I assure you, if it were up to the Chinese some days, there would be no city left."

"Get to the point," said Erdene coldly.

Damdini Sukhbaatar dangled the letter closer to Erdene until she snatched it from him and started reading. Her face was at once delight, then dread.

"You know on just what you are holding in your hands right now," said Damdini Sukhbaatar, "I could have you shot and there is nothing that the Bogd Khan could do about it. Or have you sold as some girl slave to the soldiers."

Erdene put her hand to her mouth.

The Baron

"But I am not going to do that," he added.

Damdini Sukhbaatar got up from his chair and moved to within an inch of Erdene's face. She stood frozen in fear as he slid his hands slowly across her face and neck and arm.

"No. You are going to marry me. And if you displease me or dishonour me in anyway, then your father shall be dead. And if you try and run away, I shall have you and all the priests shot."

Damdini Sukhbaatar returned to his desk and pulled out a fresh sheet of paper and a pen.

"Now, you are going to write a letter to the Russian Baron telling him that you have changed your mind and that you have no feelings for him and are to be married, so it is pointless him returning to Urga."

Erdene hesitated at first. Damdini Sukhbaatar fixes a menacing gaze.

"NOW."

Erdene blinked and then sat down, grabbing the pen and started writing.

"Dear Baron, I write with heavy heart to tell you that I do not wish to see you again. I am betrothed to another man."

******

Chapter 8

As Erdene wrote her letter, a lavish traditional Mongolian wedding feast was celebrated. At the centre of the guests was Damdini Sukhbaatar and Erdene, pretending to smile, as the shell of her father sat to the side, carefully watched by two Chinese guards.

By the time you receive this letter, we will already be happily married.

Damdini Sukhbaatar took Erdene back to a room after the feast and as Erdene resisted, Damndini slapped her across the face, causing her to fall down. He then picked her up from the floor and moved in close to kiss her. With a heart-felt sigh, Erdene stopped resisting.

Please do not make this harder than it already is by trying to contact me again as I will not write or wish to see you again.

****

Austrian-Hungarian Front

Midst, the dead, the dying and the injured at the Austrian-Hungarian Front, the Baron, looking weary and drawn was reading Erdene's letter intensely. In the distance were the figures of two Buddhist monks shuffling away.

The distraught Baron threw the letter into the fire. He stood up and paced around, with his hands on his head, before he sat back down and pulled out his service revolver. As the Baron looked up, with the service revolver still resting on his lap, he saw both Semyonov and Rezukhin running toward him. Semyonov was carrying a bottle. He put his revolver back in its holster, composing himself just as they arrive.

"Comrade, it is over!"

The Baron looked at them strangely.

"The Tsar has abdicated," said Rezukhin. "We are going home. The war at least for Russia has ended."

Semyonov pulled the top off the bottle and took a gulp before handing it to Rezukhin. The Baron shook his head.

"You are wrong Grigory Mikhaylovich," replied the Baron. "The war for Russia is only just beginning."

Chapter 9

St. Petersburg, 1917

The city of St. Petersburg no longer looked pristine, but was covered in a grey-grime as uncollected garbage and refuse piled up along the streets. People hurried along the streets, careful not to make eye contact.

The Literary Cafe itself was full of people, speaking over one another, smoking and drinking. As if nothing had changed. At a table was Semyonov and the Baron both still in military uniform and Maurice Janin, trying to be polite while sipping a coffee. Elmore Taggart moved over to the table accompanied with Alexander Kolchak.

"Brothers, let me introduce Alexander Kolchak," said Elmore Taggart, before pointing at Semyonov and the Baron. "This is Grigory Mikhaylovich Semyonov and Baron Roman Nikolai Maximilian von Ungern-Sternberg. And of course you already know Maurice."

"Yes," replied Alexander Kolchak.

Alexander Kolchak sipped his coffee before looking at Maurice Janin, ignoring Semyonov and the Baron.

"Prince Lvov and Alexander Kerensky are living in a fantasy," grumbled Alexander Kolchak. "We have no military strength anymore and without assistance from the Allied Powers, Russia will be swallowed by hungry wolves."

"I can vouch for the Czech Legionnaires," said Maurice Janin.

"And I for the Americans and Japanese," added Elmore Taggart, before looking at the Baron. "No offence to you Baron."

The Baron shook his head negatively.

"What happens then when we agree to such forces coming onto Russian soil?" asked the Baron. "Is this not the Trojan Horse we first feared?"

"You may be a good soldier Baron," replied Alexander Kolchak. "But you are no politician. The reality is we must have such support if we are to survive."

Alexander Kolchak stood up and shook the hand of Maurice Janin and then Elmore Taggart.

"I accept your proposal and I speak for all true Russians that we will resist the forces of anarchy."

Alexander Kolchak then picked up his coffee and raised it as if making a toast. The rest of the men looked slightly embarrassed until Maurice Janin stood up also with his coffee and then Elmore Taggart and finally Semyonov and the Baron with their tea.

Chapter 9

"To Russia!"

"May she survive the winter," mumbled the Baron to Semyonov.

The men collectively clink their cups and sit back down. All except the Baron.

"Gentlemen, it is an honour," said the Baron. "But I must be leaving."

The Baron extended his hand to Alexander Kolchak who shook it firmly.

"Do not go too far Baron. Your duty to mother Russia shall soon be calling."

The Baron nodded to Alexander Kolchak, Elmore Taggart and to Maurice Janin, before turning and walking toward the cafe exit.

****

The Baron stepped outside the cafe and had only covered a short distance before Semyonov bounded out of the cafe after him.

"So it is going to be like that then."

The Baron kept walking a few more steps, not bothering to turn around.

"If you want to be a politician or oligarch fine, that's your business," replied the Baron.

"So you're just going to keep walking away from your friend."

The Baron stopped and turned around to look at Semyonov and spotted Elmore Taggart had also left the cafe walking toward them.

"Grigory Mikhaylovich, Alexander Kolchak is a peacock who is selling out true Russia," added the Baron. "He hasn't got a clue and he will lose."

Elmore Taggart was now almost upon both men.

"Then help him and guide him, please!" said Semyonov

"There is something I must do -"

"What chase after that girl again in Mongolia," added Semyonov interrupting him. "She is gone. You said it yourself - "

The Baron swung around and stared at Semyonov with a look of intense anger.

"Sorry to interrupt," smiled Elmore Taggart, signalling to the Baron. "I wanted to speak with you in private."

Semyonov looked at Elmore Taggart and then at the Baron, who composes himself.

"I trust Semyonov with my life," said the Baron.

Semyonov smiled.

"So you should. I saved it enough times."

Chapter 9

"I couldn't tell you in there," added Elmore Taggart, "because Kolchak sees him as a bit of a competitor, but Pyotr Nikolayevich Wrangel has been captured by the Communist terrorists."

"Where?" asked the Baron.

"Odessa. Look, Edmund Ironside has some people down that way who can help you. I know you consider him a friend and a good general. I just thought you should know."

"So off to war against the communist terrorists then?" grinned Semyonov. "I suppose it is as good a reason as any. Unless you have other plans Baron?"

The Baron shook his head negatively.

"Good," smiled Semyonov, "then let us go and kill some Communists!"

The Baron

Chapter 10

Wrangel House, Odessa Shoreline

Wrangel, was sitting on a beautiful terrace overlooking the Black Sea, playing chess with a young Red Army Platoon Leader (Mikhail Volkov). A Red Army Company Commander (Dimitry Petrov) and several other Communist Soldiers were also sitting around, reading books or playing cards.

Wrangel watched as the young Platoon Leader moved his piece.

"You play well Mikhail," smiled Wrangel. "Your commander should be worried. Maybe you will take his place."

Collective laughter broke out among the communist troops as the commander Dimitry Petrov frowned.

"Chess is bourgeois," he growled. "I did not have time to waste on such things as a farmer. If I had my way, it would be outlawed."

Wrangel shook his head negatively.

"Dimitry, I respect there are and were many evils in society. But chess and education is not one of them."

Wrangel moved his piece.

"Tell me Mikhail, do you honestly believe in the notion that everyone will be equal under socialism?"

"Of course," said Mikhail Volkov enthusiastically. "Once you rid the world of the evils of capitalism and the greed of private property, then we may all work to the common good."

Wrangel started laughing.

"You cannot truly believe that Mikhail? Clearly you are educated and so you must know that societies don't run themselves. So what you are saying is that you would rather be ruled by an unaccountable ruling elite of intelligensia, that know nothing of administration, than an administration with centuries of experience in need of reform?"

"No, no that is not what I am saying," frowned Mikhail.

"You do know that Karl Marx simply invented Capitalism as a dialectic to promote his own insane philosophy?"

In the background there was the sound of gun fire and then two explosions. The Company Commander and the soldiers stood up. Commander Dimitry Petrov looked at Mikhail Volkov and some of the other troops nearby. "Wait here," commanded Volkov to the other troops. The Red Army officers hurried back into the building.

"Don't be too long, we have a game to finish," yelled Wrangel. "Otherwise, I will have to find someone else to play."

There was more sounds of gun fire and explosions nearby, yet Wrangel still did not flinch.

Suddenly Mikhail Volkov returned to the balcony, with his left arm injured. He raised his gun at Wrangel.

"I am sorry General. I have orders."

Yet before he could fire, there was a hail of bullets and Volkov and the other Red Army soldiers drop to the ground dead.

Wrangel then got up and surveyed the damaged wall and shattered windows of the house, just as the Baron, followed by Semyonov, Veselovskii, Sipailov and Rezukhin appeared.

Wrangel shook his head negatively, ignoring them for a moment, still reviewing the damage.

"Wrangel, are you not happy to see us?" asked Semyonov.

"Look at the damage! You destroyed my house," complained Wrangel.

"But we rescued you," said Veselovskii.

"Why? I was perfectly happy."

The Baron

Wrangel nodded and acknowledged the Baron who briefly smiled in return.

"Well, whatever," said Semyonov. "We will build you a brand new Duma. In the meantime, we have orders to get to Chita. Kolchak is poised to declare a republic."

Wrangel huffed and departed with them.

Chapter 11

Chita, 1918

A bustling scene of organised chaos outside the main railway station of Chita. White Russian soldiers pour in and out of the station while there was almost a complete absence of civilians. Midst the bustle, the Baron, Wrangel and Semyonov arrived, pushing their way past the troops.

A few streets away, the Baron, Wrangel and Semyonov arrived by foot outside a heavily guarded cinder block building. The troops saluted and the men enter the building.

Inside, Alexander Kolchak was leaning over a map on a long board room table, in an art-deco office with several other White Russian commanders, as The Baron, Wrangel and Semyonov arrive.

"It is worse than St. Petersburg at Christmas here," grumbled Semyonov.

Muffled laughter as Kolchak remains stone faced. Alexander Kolchak made eye contact with Wrangel and they nod in acknowledgement of one another.

"Baron, I am promoting you to Major General, said Alexander Kolchak. "You will be in charge with coordinating new military units around Dauria and Irkutsk while Major General Semyonov is to command the east in Siberia."

The Baron nodded and smiled at Semyonov.

"Major General," said the Baron.

"Major General," replied Semyonov.

They looked back at Alexander Kolchak who was not smiling.

"The Communists have concentrated their forces near Yakut. Major General Semyonov, your forces and division will command the east and Siberia, with assistance from the Americans."

Semyonov nodded approvingly. Kolchak then looked to Wrangel.

"Major General Wrangel, you will command our southern forces."

Wrangel nodded as Kolchak looked to the Baron.

"And Major General Ungern-Sternberg you will be tasked in pulling together all the different militias of tribes, cultures, religions and races to defend our western flanks."

The Baron nodded and smiled approvingly.

"Ungern-Sternberg your commanders are outside the city waiting for you. These Russians, Buryats, Tatars, Bashkirs, Mongols all need to be united under one purpose: to stopping the communists. Your division is to be called the 1st Asiatic Cavalry. And you are authorised to use whatever force or tactics are necessary to stop the Communists from cutting Russia in half."

"Then may God have mercy on the communists," chuckled Semyonov. "Because no one has ever given Baron Roman Nikolai Maximilian von Ungern-Sternberg the power to do whatever he needs to win."

****

1st Asiatic Cavalry HQ, Dauria, 1918

The Baron arrived with an escort to a non-descript building outside of Chita. Outside the building, he was formally greeted and saluted by Sipailov, Rezukhin and Veselovskii.

"Welcome Major General," smiled Sipailov, followed by Rezukhin and Veselovskii.

The Baron laughed. "They told me my commanders would be waiting for me," he said. "Not that it would take years to train them out of bad habits."

All the men laughed and embraced the Baron. A moment later, Elmore Taggart and then Edmund

The Baron

Ironside stepped out of the building. The face of the Baron lit up when he saw both men.

"Baron! You made it at last," grinned Elmore Taggart.

They shook hands and embraced before the Baron also acknowledged Edmund Ironside.

"Thank you for the help with rescuing Wrangel," said the Baron.

"I am glad we could be of service," smiled Edmund Ironside. "Taggart and I agreed that if neither of us could recruit you, the least we could do is see you have a decent go of it against the Communists."

Sipailov signalled for the Baron to follow him into the headquarters.

"Come, let us show you what you have inherited."

When the Baron stepped inside, the officers and staff stand to attention. On the walls were maps of the regions, including Mongolia, with a summary of names, commands and sources of the Division. Sipailov stepped forward to the map of the Division and began pointing to different units and names.

"Major General, your Division is made up of approximately three thousand men as two brigades and a support regiment," said Sipailov. "The first brigade is led by myself -"

"And the second by me," smiled Rezukhin.

The Baron slapped his head. "God help me."

"I am commanding the support regiment," smiled Veselovskii. "We have some great tools, thanks to our friends here today."

"I am sorry, we could not do more," said Edmund Ironside. "But technically we are not supposed to be here at all."

"We have ten aircraft, 8 British artillery pieces and 20 Japanese machine gun teams," said Veselovskii.

The Baron smiled.

"The best I could do Baron," grinned Elmore Taggart.

"No, no. It is excellent," replied the Baron. He looked around the room. "I would like the Division to be ready for inspection before the end of today, when I will address them, before we move out."

The commanders saluted, as the Baron stepped out of the headquarters followed by his commanders, Edmund Ironside and Elmore Taggart.

Taggart moved up next to the Baron. "The powers-that-be are nervous backing the wrong team," he said. "They like you but are not so sure Kolchak will survive. If things swing the other way, there is nothing I can do."

The Baron

The Baron nodded. "I understand. Let me put to best use what you have given me and we shall see what can be done."

****

The Baron on horseback, rode along the line of Cossacks and soldiers in position. He stopped at the centre of where his commanders had assembled and began his speech.

"I know all of you assembled here today are volunteers and patriots. Christian, Jew, Muslim, Buddhist and Taoist. Russian, Tartar, Mongol, Turkic, Uralic, Buryat and Japanese. Every religion. Every race of Asiatic peoples. Truly, before me is the truth that no force in heaven or upon the earth can deny. We have come together not because we wish for the old ways of the past, but because we sense the real danger and evil facing our future. Socialism, communism is not a true philosophy. Instead it is an array of slogans for the quest of naked power. Power by any means. Power, no matter how evil an act. Let there be no doubt, that if we fail, then our children and descendants will be enslaved by a force of evil the likes of which has not been seen before. Here then be our choice. Every man and woman eventually dies. This is the way of the universe. But all of us here now have a choice. Let this be the time we stand up against the face of evil. I will not abandon you, nor betray your loyalty. Let it be for a cause greater than ourselves."

At the conclusion of the speech, there was a collective roar from the soldiers.

****

Yakut, 1918

Yakut was a city smouldering and traumatized from recent battle. All semblance of colour vanquished from its streets, midst the ruins and piles of bodies of the unknown. The Asiatic Cavalry escorted lines of prisoners into the city, while injured White Russian troops were carefully carried out in the other direction.

The Baron, accompanied by Rezukhin entered the remains of the city square. Around the edges of the square, Asiatic Cavalry soldiers were busily tearing down every communist flag they could find and replacing them with the Imperial Russian flags. In front of the Baron, a group of several hundred

Communist prisoners were sitting on the ground, with their hands tied as soldiers guard them.

"Casualties?" asked the Baron.

"One hundred and forty two dead and three hundred and fifty wounded," replied Rezukhin. "About a hundred critically."

"And the enemy?"

"We haven't done a complete count yet, but about two thousand dead and not counting these ones, around three and a half thousand prisoners."

Rezukhin pointed to a building to the right of them that had not been destroyed.

"That is the building the Division priest wants as a temporary church," he said. "But the Rabbi also wants it as a Synagogue and is fighting with the Islamic Imam."

"Let them work it out between themselves or no one is getting it," replied the Baron.

Leonid Sipailov stepped up to the Baron and saluted. He pointed to the prisoners in front of them in the square.

"These ones we found in the main Communist Party Headquarters," he said. "What do you want me to do with them?"

"I want to see them first," said the Baron.

Chapter 11

The Baron walked along the line of prisoners. Face after face of utter resignation or blank nothingness. The Baron stopped and looked at one prisoner, who kept his head completely down, hiding his face.

"That one," said the Baron, pointing to the prisoner.

Sipailov motioned to one of the guards.

"Prisoner, show your face," said the guard.

Slowly the prisoner lifted his face to reveal it was a dirty and haggard Minei Gubelman.

"Minei!" yelled the Baron.

Minei Gubelman ignored him and put his head back down.

"Minei, it is you," said the Baron. "Show me your face and say something!"

After a moment, Minei raised his face and stared with contempt at the Baron. "My name is Yemelyan Mikhailovich Yaroslavsky and if it be your decision, then I shall die with my comrades."

The Baron began laughing, causing some of the soldiers to also laugh, without the soldiers knowing the reason.

"Release him and bring him to my office," said the Baron.

"And the others?" asked Sipailov.

"You know what to do. But give them a proper burial."

Leonid Sipailov saluted as the Baron turned and walked away.

****

Asiatic Cavalry HQ, Yakut

The Baron was inside a spacious office, with an attendant standing next to him holding a clean shirt and towel. The Baron took off his shirt to reveal the khata scarf stained red with blood. He threw the shirt off and placed the blood stained khata over a chair, next to a beautifully ornate desk, before washing his face and hands. As he began to put on the clean shirt, there was a firm knock at the door.

"Enter," said the Baron.

Minei Gubelman escorted by two guards entered the room, as the Baron finished wrapping the blood stained khata around his neck.

"It is fine," said the Baron to the guards. "You can leave us."

The guards initially hesitated, before saluting and leaving.

Chapter 11

The Baron got up and walked over to a side table and grabbed two glasses and a bottle. Minei remained standing as the Baron placed the glasses and bottle on the desk and sat down on a chair.

"I do not need your hospitality, growled Minei," while looking straight ahead. "Nor will I betray the Glorious Peoples Revolution."

The Baron started laughing.

"Stop. Stop, Minei. you will make me break a rib from laughing."

The Baron composed himself, and poured two glasses, as Minei remained standing and looking straight ahead, without making eye contact.

"My name is not Minei, it is Yemelyan Mikhai -"

The Baron waved his hand as he placed a glass on the desk in front of Minei.

"Yes, yes, I heard you the first time." The Baron clinked his glass against the glass of Minei Gubelman. "To our inevitable deaths."

The Baron gulped down the vodka, before returning to the other side of the desk, as Minei eventually looked at him and slowly reached for the vodka and sipped his drink.

"I have seen the headless corpses of men, who had been sitting twenty miles from the front who were killed simply by mishap," said the Baron. "And I have seen men run naked through a minefield, completely mad, yet without a scratch. So you tell me then when we die?"

"I am not afraid to die," said Minei. "Especially for the future of the proletariat."

"Can you hear yourself?" smiled the Baron. "You have simply swapped the identity of royalty for the cult of the revolutionary identity. Nothing more."

Minei scowled at the Baron.

"I know who you really are Bloody Baron. I know all about your obsession in mysticism and murder."

The Baron shook his head and moved back to his desk, selecting a form on his desk. "Ah, yes the lies of Kamenev and his *Pravda*," he said. "You used to be a man of intellect, even if a bit stuck up. What caused you to abandon all sense of common sense and reason?"

"I vow that before this war is over, the glorious proletariat of the people shall have the last laugh," said Minei defiantly.

The Baron looked down and finished signing a piece of paper.

"Maybe you will. Maybe you won't. But it won't be by my hands," said the Baron. "Guards," he yelled.

"Minei, you are not a soldier. As much as you love your revolution."

The guards burst into the office as the Baron stood up and handed the papers to them.

"Take this man to the outskirts of the city. Make sure he has supplies and civilian clothes and then set him free."

Minei Gubelman looked stunned.

"Good luck Minei."

The Baron

Chapter 12

Urga

Erdene, followed a cart, carrying a body wrapped in white and accompanied by four Buddhist monks as Damdini Sukhbaatar pushes past them to reach her. Erdene slapped him hard across the face.

"You promised," she sobbed.

"It is not my fault," protested Damdini Sukhbaatar.

"You promised and now my father is dead."

Damndini grabbed her arm but she pushed him away. "Don't touch me," she said. "Don't you ever touch me again."

Erdene wiped away her tears, before looking directly at Damdini Sukhbaatar with cold resolute intent. "I may be your wife. But you are dead to me and I will not sleep with you or attend you again. "

Damdini Sukhbaatar stopped walking and stepped aside, letting the cart and Erdene and the Buddhist monks continue down the dirt road.

****

Dauria Battlefield

The Baron was standing on a stool, gruesomely orchestrating his soldiers in the stringing up of the dead bodies of Communists on stakes. Watching on, was Sipailov and Rezukhin.

"Why do you do all this?" asked Sipailov. "It seems such a huge waste of effort when we could just let the bodies rot."

The Baron laughed.

"Propaganda Leonidivich," he said. "The Communists think they are the best propagandists, but everyone remembers the stories of Vlad the Impaler."

"But these soldiers are already dead," added Rezukhin, "whereas Vlad was supposed to have impaled people alive."

"Borisovich how many enemy soldiers did we kill in the last three months alone?"

Rezukhin looked at Sipailov and then back at the Baron.

"I have lost count. Maybe eight to ten thousand," said Rezukhin

"And Leonidivich how many men have we lost?"

"Over four hundred," said Sipailov.

Chapter 12

"So given we are replenishing our units at roughly half what we have lost, how much longer before we will cease to be capable of operating as a Division, even if we kill thirty thousand more communists?"

"I see your point," said Sipailov

"Let the enemies imagination run wild. So much the better for us if they think they are fighting the Devil himself."

The Baron stepped off the stool and waved for the soldiers to finish.

He surveyed the road into the distance. A long line of hundreds and hundreds of bodies impaled on stakes lining either side of the road as far as the eye could see.

****

Chita, 1919

The Baron walked alone to the heavily guarded cinder block headquarters of the White forces.

Inside, Wrangel, Semyonov and several other officers were already in discussion. Kolchak was pre-occupied in another corner, trying out a new uniform with a tailor. Wrangel was the first to spot the Baron as he entered.

The Baron

"Your reputation has grown since the last time we met," grinned Wrangel.

"Baron Pyotr Nikolayevich you know better than most. War is hell and one must do what he can to unsettle the enemy," smiled the Baron.

"Ah here he is, the Bloody Baron! Baron von Blood," proclaimed Semyonov.

"Don't believe everything you read Grigory Mikhaylovich," replied the Baron.

"Pulling us out of the field for this meeting is a big gamble for Kolchak," said Semyonov. "What have you heard?"

"That you are even a bigger drinker and womaniser now than you ever were," grinned the Baron.

General laughter as Alexander Kolchak stepped over in his new uniform.

"The French have betrayed us," frowned Kolchak. "The Czech Legionnaires are pulling out on orders of Maurice Janin."

"What about the Americans?" asked Wrangel. "Surely they don't want to see the Communists take over."

"As far as I can tell, they are playing both sides so whoever comes out on top is obligated. I leave for a meeting tonight in the hope of persuading the

Chapter 12

Americans and British to help defend the Russian Republic, which is why I call you all here," said Kolchak. "I am putting Grigory Mikhaylovich Semyonov in charge until my return."

"Then God help us," sighed the Baron.

Semyonov punched the Baron on the arm.

"Careful. I might just send you on a mission to Moscow," grinned Semyonov.

"That is all," said Kolchak.

The generals saluted as Alexander Kolchak left the room.

****

Chita, Railway Station

Semyonov, the Baron and Wrangel were standing out in front of the railway station, surrounded by a cordon of soldiers.

"So what do you think?" said Semyonov to the Baron.

"I don't like it," said the Baron. "I think it is a trap. But with the Czech Legionnaires gone, we have a huge hole in our south and western flank."

The Baron

From the entrance of the train station, two Buddhist monks approached.

"What about you Wrangel?" asked Semyonov.

"I am a soldier, not a martyr," replied Wrangel. "I'll take my divisions into the gap and hold as best I can and pray that the Americans and British pull through."

As the two Buddhist monks were almost upon the guards surrounding the generals, Semyonov spotted them and started shaking his head, while prodding the Baron.

"What is it with you and Buddhist monks walking into hell?"

"And how do they keep finding you?" asked Wrangel.

The Baron shrugged his shoulders and motioned to the guards to let the two Buddhist monks pass through. The Baron bowed to the monks and the monks bowed to him. They handed him a letter beautifully wrapped in gold leaf. As soon as they handed over the letter, the monks bowed and departed.

"Fancy," smiled Semyonov. "Who is it?"

The Baron opened the letter and started scratching his head.

"It is from the Bogd Khan," replied the Baron.

"Who?" asked Wrangel.

"Some sharman the Baron met when he was in love in Mongolia," grinned Semyonov.

The Baron darted a deadly stare at Semyonov who paused for a moment, before the Baron calmed.

"What does it say?" asked Semyonov.

"It just says *Everything yields but the heart. Remember your promise.*"

"See," said Semyonov, "that is why I never follow sharmans."

"He is the second to the Dalai Lama and considered a living incarnation of Buddha," added the Baron.

The Baron embraced Wrangel before turning and started to walk away.

"Hey!" yelled Semyonov. "I am in charge now. Where are you going?"

"To fulfil a promise," said the Baron.

The Baron

Chapter 13

Duma Above Urga

High above the city of Urga, on the stone steps of the ancient Duma, Erdene sat alone.

"I am sorry it took me so long to finally get here," said a voice from behind her.

Erdene, was shocked at hearing the voice. She swung around to look for its source.

"Who is this? Why do you still torment me?"

"It is only me," said the Baron. "Roman Nikolai."

The Baron stepped out from behind a pillar, holding a bunch of flowers. In the instant Erdene saw his face, she rushed over and fell into his arms, weeping.

"Oh how I have dreamt of this," she said, sobbing.

They embrace for a time until Erdene pushed back, with first a look of perplexity and then fear.

"But the guards? How could this be?" she asked. "Am I dead, is this only a dream."

The Baron smiled and moved forward again, kissing her hand.

"The Chinese guards have been taken care of," he said. "You have nothing to fear. I have been watching the city for eight days now. Waiting and hoping for this moment. You are safe now."

Erdene kissed him passionately on the lips, before Erdene once again broke the embrace and looked at the Baron.

"You have changed," she said.

"War does that."

The Baron revealed the prayer beads around his arm and then the off coloured khata still around his neck. No longer blood red, nor white.

Erdene smiled, before she frowned.

"He made me write that letter. Damdini Sukhbaatar," she grumbled. "He is very dangerous and will not stop."

"Do not worry. I did not come alone."

The Baron took Erdene by the hand and escorted her to the other side of Duma. Hidden from the view of the Chinese, Erdene saw the faces of many hundreds of soldiers of the 1st Cavalary Division.

"But there are thousands of Chinese soldiers," she said.

"That won't stop my men," smiled the Baron.

****

Chapter 13

Damdini Sukhbaatar House

Damdini Sukhbaatar stomped through the gates of the former home of the Prime Minister, to be greeted by the salutes of the Chinese guards.

"Where is she?" he demanded to one of the guards.

The guard shrugged nervously as Damndini brushed past and stepped into the building.

Inside, he burst through door after door, looking for her. He checked her clothes and personal items. He even looked under the beds and in the closets as the attendants watched on anxiously. In one room, in a fit of fury, Damdini Sukhbaatar screamed and smashed a mirror on the wall before upturning all the furniture.

Two soldiers rushed in to see if Damdini Sukhbaatar was hurt.

"Find her!" he yelled. "Take everyone and find her."

****

Mountains Above Urga

The Baron and Erdene were sitting at the site of a camp fire, high in the mountains, as troops surround them just outside the light of the fire. The Baron poked a stick into the fire and embers swirled up into the night sky.

"You fought in that terrible war?" asked Erdene.

The Baron nodded.

"Was it as bad as they say?"

"Worse," he said softly. "But it is over now."

Erdene smiled.

"It seems we all change."

The Baron shook his head negatively.

"Not you," he said "You are still as beautiful as I first remember."

Erdene shook her head negatively.

"No. He forced me to marry him. He killed my father. He changed me."

The Baron reached over and cuddled Erdene.

"His day will come, soon enough," he said.

****

The silhouette of Chinese secret police on horseback against the moonlight, as they wind up the pass, closer to the Cossack camp.

****

Chapter 13

The Baron covered Erdene with a blanket to keep her warm.

"So what will you do? The Chinese have many men and machine guns and artillery."

The Baron smiled.

"Get some rest. In the morning we shall plan our attack and surprise them -"

At that moment, there was the sound of gun shots in the background, followed by a volley of gunfire going off.

The baron sprung up and grabbed a rifle, as Rezukhin came running over.

"It is a patrol from the city," said Rezukhin.

"Don't let any escape," said the Baron.

Rezukhin swung around and returned toward the sound of the firing. The Baron looked back to see Erdene hurrying toward him. He put his hand up.

"Stay here," he said. "It is too dangerous."

"No less dangerous for you," she replied.

****

The Baron, followed by Erdene approach the position of Rezukhin and the troops, as they continue to exchange gunfire with the Chinese police officers.

The Baron

A few moments later, after the volley of shots from the Cossacks, the guns of the Secret Police fall silent. The Baron approached Rezukhin.

"Is that all of them?" asked the Baron.

"I think so," said Rezukhin as Erdene stepped over. She pointed down into the valley and the distant shapes of two riders at full gallop heading towards the main security checkpoint of the city.

"There is your answer," she said.

"There goes our element of surprise," grinned Rezukhin.

Chapter 14

Duma Above Urga

In the ancient Duma overlooking Urga, the Baron and his commanders studied a map of the city.

"Xu Shuzheng has approximately ten and half thousand troops dug into positions around the city," said Sipailov. "The heaviest lines are against any kind of frontal assault to cross the river. His artillery is positioned to his left and right flanks guarding access from the valley. But the problem is, at least half his forces are embedded with the population."

"Even if we charge at speed, there is no way to get to the edge of the city without being exposed for several minutes in range of their artillery and machine guns," said Rezukhin.

"I know you are concerned about casualties with our men," said Veselovskii. "The simplest is still to shell the city like our normal plan."

The Baron shook his head negatively.

"We are not going to burn the city," he said. "I want the population unharmed."

"Then you could lose half our forces in urban fighting alone Baron," said Rezukhin.

The Baron shook his head negatively. "We don't have to sacrifice men comrades, we just need to come up with a plan that unsettles them and plays with their minds," grinned the Baron. "Then, and only then will we attack."

"Yes," added Rezukhin, "Unlike the Red Army, we have time on our side. It will take weeks for the Chinese to send reinforcements."

"Then let us make sure that the last thing the Chinese will want to do is send more troops here," replied the Baron.

Sipailov smiled. "I wonder if they have heard of the Bloody Baron?"

****

A rag-tag looking troop of what looked like some 60 marauders approached the front lines of the Chinese outside Urga. At 400 yards, the Chinese started to open fire and the marauders, rode away.

Soon after, a unit of Chinese cavalry of over 200 rode out of Urga to chase after them.

The Chinese cavalry pursued the apparent marauders high up into the mountains and over the pass, until on the other side, they were surrounded by the rest of the Baron's men and captured.

****

It was night, above and around Urga. The Baron was standing with Erdene, watching the darkened valley below.

"I am not what you are going to see me have to do," said the Baron. "There is no other way to save your people. Please forgive me."

Erdene smiled and kissed him. "I know who you are. Do not worry," she said. "In the deeper teachings of our people, such notions of good and evil are considered false and subjective distractions of the mind from the root cause of continued suffering through ignorance. A man who seeks to save the suffering of many, by doing what he considers necessary, so long as it is without the poisons of greed, ill will or delusion, cannot be considered evil."

The Baron and Erdene embraced, before the Baron stepped back.

"Even so, I wish you will not hear or see the things that we must do," he said.

The Baron

****

Around the foothills of Urga, five hundred campfires were lit, as screams of horrendous torture echoed through the night sky.

Upon morning, a grizzly and horrible sight greeted the Chinese forces, as sixty of their comrades appeared impaled upon a line of stakes, beyond their front lines.

The Chinese pulled down their dead and retreated. A few hours later, they returned and established a new ring of forward machine gun posts, as an additional wall of security.

****

As night fell around the hills and mountains surrounding Urga, the screams continued, as now one thousand camp fires were lit.

Upon morning, there were no grisly sights. Yet, the soldiers from the forward machine gun posts were missing.

As Xu Shuzheng ordered troops out to resume the forward machine gun posts, four naked and bloody Chinese riders appeared on the horizon, carrying a strange cargo. As the Chinese riders approached, yelling and screaming, one Chinese defender shot one of his own out of fright. Yet the others continued, until it could be clearly seen the cargo they were carrying were the heads of other Chinese soldiers, tied around the horses.

"The Bloody Baron is coming to kill us," they screamed. "The Devil himself is coming to drink our blood and eat our flesh," the traumatised men screamed, until they were cut loose from the horses.

****

As night fell, four thousand fires lit up the foothills and mountains surrounding Urga. No longer was the sound of screams heard, but beating drums and mad laughter and yelling echoed into the night sky.

Upon the morning, the 2nd Cavalry brigade of Rezukhin approached in single line, stretching across the valley. Behind them, the 1st Cavalry brigade of Sipailov whirled around in great circles, creating huge clouds of dust, and the illusion of a massive approaching army.

Rezukhin then gave the order to charge at full gallop, as the 1st Cavalry brigade split off from behind and used the dust cloud to move to the west flank of the city.

Before Rezukhin and his brave men and their horses had even reached the forward machine gun positions of the Chinese, the Chinese soldiers had begun abandoning their posts and running back into the city.

Only when the 2nd Cavalry brigade reached the northern outskirts of the city did some Chinese defenders begin firing. But by this stage, the 1st Cavalry brigade had breached the western defences of the city and the Chinese were in full retreat.

The Baron and his guards followed the advance of the 2nd Cavalry into the city, until he met up with Rezukhin and the final assault on the Chinese headquarters of Xu Shuzheng.

"Is Xu Shuzheng still in there do you think?" yelled the Baron, over the gunfire and smoke.

Rezukhin nodded. "Once we take care of these rats, the rest have fled," he said. "What do you want to do? We have them surrounded. We will lose less men if we sit it out and force a surrender."

The Baron shook his head negatively. "If we delay, there is a chance they may regroup, or even start using the people as shields. End it now. End it quickly."

Chapter 14

Rezukhin saluted. "Attack", he yelled and stepped forward with his men, as a mass of Cossacks stormed toward the building.

Machine gun fire cut down a number of them, before there were two huge explosions just inside the building. When the smoke cleared, the Chinese shooting stopped and the Chinese survivors began filing out of the building, under white flags.

"Cease fire," yelled Rezukhin as he stepped forward, approaching the lead Chinese exiting the damaged building.

But as he approached, some of the Chinese defenders started firing again and cut down Rezukhin and the men standing next to him.

"Fire," yelled the Baron and his men resumed firing, cutting down the Chinese that had exited the building, before using cannons to fire directly into the building.

After a few more minutes and no more Chinese gunfire, the Baron ordered his men to cease. The Baron then rushed forward to where Rezukhin had fallen. He lifted his head, but there was no use. Sobbing, the Baron cradled Rezukhin, before Sipailov came over to him and gently touched his shoulder.

The Baron

The Baron swung around and looked at Sipailov and then a steady stream of Chinese prisoners.

"When they're all out, you know what to do for the memory of our comrade Rezukhin," said the Baron.

Sipailov saluted and turned back to the soldiers guarding the surrendering Chinese prisoners.

Chapter 15

Bogd Khan Palace

The Baron was escorted by Mongolian guards through the Palace Hallway.

Inside the palace, the Baron entered the inner gardens where the Bogd Khan was sitting and smiling on the same seat where they sat and spoke years before. He signalled for the Baron to sit.

"Thank you," smiled the Bogd Khan.

"No, it is I who should be thanking you, your holiness. If not for your letter."

The Bogd Khan started laughing.

"Thus is proven the maxim, since we are in agreement, the pen is truly mightier than the sword."

"I am afraid it will not be that easy," replied the Baron. "The Chinese could launch a major counter attack any day. The Americans and Europeans have abandoned us and the Communists continue to advance and may still attack. Maybe if we have enough time, we can train five to ten thousand. But we do not have the weapons."

The Bogd Khan put up his hand.

"Surely you know the answer to the question of what is lasting? For a man taught to kill, knows only to kill or be killed and when he dies nothing remains. Yet when a man is taught to live in a civilised manner, his legacy is life and knowledge. "

"So you don't want me to train you an army?"

The Bogd Khan smiled.

"If the forces of China or the Communists are as formidable as you say, then such an act would ultimately be futile. Instead, I would rather hope you show our people how to unite with common purpose as was the miracle of you uniting so many religions and races into your army."

"But it could all end in a month or at best a year if we cannot defend ourselves."

"A crow raided a nest as is its nature. Yet in the nest it found an acorn. So the crow resolved to grab the acorn first and then the egg and fly away. Yet the seed stuck in his neck and he suffocated and dropped dead from the sky onto a field. Some years later a mighty tree grew from that seed."

"Are you saying I am that crow."

The Bogd Khan laughed loudly.

Chapter 15

"War is the crow my son. You are the seed for my people. The people already see you as the reincarnation of the Mongol God of War."

"That is not why I came your holiness," said the Baron. "I have no desire to be a ruler, much less a God."

"Yet as you just witnessed. Powerful be the symbols of our minds," replied the Bogd Khan. "You just defeated a larger and better equipped army of China, because they feared your reputation."

"What do you propose then your holiness?"

"It always struck me as odd that such powers as America, Great Britain, France and others would spend so much time fussing over this land, until I saw how much they craved its natural wealth. A strong leader could do much to speak to these powers, despite other differences, do you agree?"

The Baron nodded his head. "Yes," he said. "While my heart is for Russia, they would still see Mongolia as a separate concern."

"Then together, let us see what other miracles may come?" smiled the Bogd Khan.

****

Bogd Khan Palace

The Baron

The American Elmore Taggart and the British Major Edmund Ironside stepped warily into the great hall. At the end of the hall were now two platforms, the higher platform of the Bogd Khan and a lower platform for the Daichin Tengri, the red god of war.

An announcer, heralded their appearance. "The trade and mining representatives of the United States of America and the United Kingdom."

As Elmore Taggart and Edmund Ironside approached, they briefly locked eyes on the figure of the Baron, dressed in fine red silks, sitting on the lower platform. The Baron allowed himself the briefest of smiles.

"Oh Great Daichin Tengri," said Elmore Taggart. "We have heard astounding things about your exploits. My government brings its best wishes to the people of Mongolia and an offer of financial assistance."

"That all be very well," said the Baron. "But we have seen how temperamental this good will can be."

The Baron looked up at the smiling face of the Bogd Khan, before frowning at the sheepish looking Elmore Taggart and Edmund Ironside.

"We can assure the Daichin Tengri," said Edmund Ironside, "that the intentions of our governments for the well being of the people of Mongolia is genuine and has nothing to do with any policy toward the present civil unrest in Russia."

The Baron continued to stare at Elmore Taggart and Edmund Ironside, before looking up at the Bogd Khan and then back at the two men in front of him.

"I have decided I shall meet these men in private," said the Baron. "To see if there be honour in seeking a more fruitful relationship."

****

The Baron in his fine red silk robes was sitting on a beautiful stone seat, while Elmore Taggart and Edmund Ironside sat on the bench opposite him, within the beautiful internal gardens of the palace.

"A beautiful place your highness," said Edmund Ironside.

The Baron started laughing, causing discomfort on the faces of the men opposite.

"Why don't we all cut the act, shall we?" he said. "I know you or your bosses had Kolchak killed and are itching to back the Communists once Lenin is out of the way. Yet, I also know, I would be long dead by now, if not for the resources you both gave me."

"You're welcome," smiled Edmund Ironside.

"That's better," grinned the Baron.

Edmund Ironside looked at Elmore Taggart and back at the Baron.

"We were getting nervous if the reports about the Mad Bloody Baron were actually true," said Edmund Ironside. "And then when we heard you had been anointed the Daichin Tengri, the living red god of war, then we were really concerned."

"You know the Communists have gone completely all out against you," added Elmore Taggart. "The Pravda has made you Public Enemy No. 1 and publishes daily the horrors and evils of the Bloody Baron."

"I am flattered," smiled the Baron.

"Indeed, they even published a piece last week saying that you believed yourself to be the reincarnation of Kenghis Khan and had ordered the gruesome torture and murder of all Jews and Orthodox Christians in Urga," said Edmund Ironside.

The Baron started to laugh. "I have hundreds of Jews and thousands of Christian soldiers under my command, as well as Hindu, Buddhists and others," he said. "The Bolshevik propaganda has become absurd."

"Yet, some will believe," said Elmore Taggart.

Chapter 15

"Yet not your governments, because you came," said the Baron. "And that is all that matters."

The Baron stood up for a moment, and spun around, touching on the leaves of the nearby plants, before looking at both of the men opposite him.

"I know for many that I am an enigma. That is true even to myself. Yet, I am neither a fool, or delusional. I know my time is limited. To the Chinese, I represent an enemy that they must find a way to extinguish one way or another. Yet to the Communists, I am the very personification of evil. I am the very being they use to frighten their own soldiers and enslaved population into submission. My death and destruction is written into the very purpose of their mission. Yet for the time being, I find myself effectively the dictator of a small country with vast mineral and strategic wealth. So how do we proceed?"

Elmore Taggart smiled. "My government has authorised me to offer your government the latest military aid and equipment you need -"

The Baron waved his hand, cutting Taggart off from speaking.

"Stop, stop," he said. "It is me who you are talking with. Not Kolchak or some half baked ego-maniac. Let me make it clearer for you. I don't want Mongolia taken over by the Communists as an extension of their reach. And I don't want China either to seize control. Yet, this country has no electricity, no hospitals, no schools, no paved roads, no sanitation plants or clean drinking water. But it has a lot of valuable minerals. So I ask again, how do you wish to proceed?"

"Well Baron," grinned Elmore Taggart. "We have some of the best utility and engineering companies in the world. I am sure we could get started right away on a number of projects to benefit the people of Mongolia and its future."

Chapter 16

The Baron's Headquarters, 1922

The Russian Asiatic guards saluted Sipailov as he entered the former secret police headquarters.

Inside, the Baron, in his simple Cossack uniform, was signing documents, when there was a firm knock on the door.

"Enter," he said crisply as Sipailov entered, holding papers.

The Baron looked up and smiled.

"Any news from Chita?" he asked.

Sipailov shook his head negatively.

"Chita is lost," said Sipailov. "The Red Army under Henrich Christoforovich Eiche was simply too great. They kept sending in wave after wave of poor souls until our men ran out of bullets."

"And Semyonov?"

"Grigory Mikhaylovich has withdrawn the government and remaining army to Vladivostok. He is still trying to negotiate with the Americans for support."

The Baron put his head in his hands.

"Wrangel did manage to evacuate with some refugees through Crimea," added Sipailov. "He has made it to Croatia. But the war is over for him."

The Baron stood up and started to pace the room.

"The only good news I can report is that we successfully captured the key leadership of the Communist Mongolian terrorists," smiled Sipailov. "We have Damdini Sukhbaatar and four of his associated in prison now. Do you want them interrogated before we execute them?"

The Baron waved his hand negatively.

"Leave them alone," he said. "Don't touch them. I will come over and see Damdini Sukhbaatar myself."

Sipailov nodded.

"But what about Erdene and this news?" he added. "She has wanted this man executed since we first arrived?"

"I will speak with Erdene," said the Baron. "Leonidivich, time is running out. We cannot win against a monster such as the Red Army that is prepared to throw millions of conscripts against us. We have to think of what can survive after we are gone."

****

Chapter 16

The Baron entered the prison, to the surprise of the guards. He saluted crisply, before the commandant Colonel Lavrentyev stepped forward and saluted the Baron.

"I wish to see the prisoner Damdini Sukhbaatar," said the Baron.

The colonel signalled for the Baron to follow him. They stopped outside a cell, as a guard opened the door.

"I will speak with the prisoner alone," said the Baron and the guard stepped back, before the Baron entered the cell.

Inside, Damdini Sukhbaatar stood up when the Baron stepped inside the cell.

"I trust you are not hungry or cold?" asked the Baron.

The face of Damdini Sukhbaatar was a mix of fear and confusion.

"I do not understand? Why would the devil treat me this way?" said Damdini Sukhbaatar. "Or is this a trick or some mind game?"

The Baron shook his head negatively.

"No game. We no longer have time for games."

"Does Erdene know that I am here?"

"I will speak with her later," said the Baron.

The Baron

Damdini Sukhbaatar smiled. "If you do not wish to kill me yet, she surely will."

"You no doubt know that the Americans have installed one of their own, the former priest named Joseph Stalin, to succeed Lenin."

Damdini Sukhbaatar shrugged his shoulders.

"With American banks now owning and financing the Communist experiment into a giant slave factory to be known as the Socialist Soviet, it is only a matter of time, before they come here."

Damdini Sukhbaatar smiled.

"Then my death would not have been in vain."

The Baron shook his head.

"Why is it every revolutionary and every socialist I have ever met is so quick to want to throw away their life for a lie?"

Damdini Sukhbaatar looked at the Baron defiantly.

"You will not break me," he said. No matter what mind games you seek to play."

"Look Sukhbaatar," said the Baron in frustration. "I am not going to execute you, or your comrades. Instead, I want you to be ready."

Damdini Sukhbaatar look confused.

"Thanks to the European and America powers, Mongolia now has an electricity grid, sanitation, free schools and hospitals and its first roads. Everything you say you want to give the Mongolian people as a socialist, yes?"

Damdini Sukhbaatar nodded his head.

"But if the Red or Soviet Army of a million men under Henrich Christoforovich Eiche turns to Mongolia, without some organised future, then nothing will be left," said the Baron. And I mean nothing. A complete wasteland."

"What do you propose then?" asked Damdini Sukhbaatar.

"The first is easy," smiled the Baron. "A prisoner that survived the cruel and evil Bloody Baron. That is an award that any Chinese military leader or even the highest party leader in Moscow would love to have. The hard part is learning the politics."

"So what do you want from me?"

"Do not harm Erdene, even if she is spiteful to you. Do not harm the Bogd Khan. And most of all, do not harm the people of Mongolia."

The Baron

Chapter 17

Inside the former family home of Erdene, the Baron was finishing packing his kit and his minimal personal possessions. Erdene burst into the room and strode over to him, slapping him hard across the face.

"I was going to tell you that we picked him up the other week," he said.

Erdene shook her head, trying to control her rising tears.

"I don't care about Damdini Sukhbaatar. He is dead to me," she said. "I care about you. How could you do this to me and leave me?"

Erdene began to sob as the Baron stepped over to comfort her. She resisted at first and then allowed him to embrace her.

"The last thing I want to do is leave you and this place," he said. "The past two years have been the happiest of my life-"

"Then stay," she cried, interrupting him. "I need you. Don't leave me again."

"Erdene I love you. I fell in love with you the moment I first saw you. And I will never stop loving you. But if I stay, then the whole Red Army of over a million soldiers will come here and destroy everything

I love. So if I leave now, then maybe I can save you and this most beautiful land."

"Yet you are the great Daichin Tengri, the red god of war," she sobbed. "You have destroyed enemies twenty times your size."

The Baron shook his head negatively.

"This is different now," he said. "They have made me the personification of everything they fear and hate. I am their ultimate nemesis. Their armies of hundreds of thousands of men march to songs about the evils of the Bloody Baron and their single minded goal is my destruction. I cannot win."

"But you must," she cried, hitting his chest. "Please, you must stay."

The Baron pulled away. "I cannot."

Erdene wiped her tears.

"Then I refuse to see you go," she said defiantly. "You have said you are leaving, so goodbye."

She turned and stomped out of the room, while the Baron paused, before finishing packing.

****

The Bogd Khan was sitting reading on the seat in the gardens as the Baron approached.

"I will miss these gardens," smiled the Baron

"They will miss you."

"When the last forces of the Republic fall, it is only a matter of time. If I stay, the Communists will surely come and destroy the city."

The Bogd Khan smiled. "You have done everything you could," he said.

"I have put Leonid Sipailov in charge of defences," said the Baron. "But if the city is surrounded, he will not let the city be destroyed in a siege. Damdini Sukhbaatar and his men are safe and will not be harmed."

The Bogd Khan nodded his head. "You have thought of everything," he smiled.

"No, Not everything," replied the Baron.

"Ah, yes, I see. The mind turns to the legacy of a man who has given so much and lived so humbly," said the Bogd Khan. "The way anyone learns may be difficult. The cuts and bruises of life and especially the wounded heart. Yet it is nothing compared to the collective suffering of peoples as a community or nation or species. Do not fear the falsities and slanderous wickedness they shall speak of your name. In time, the truth of what you did for the people of

Mongolia and all the peoples of the great plains will be known."

"I am at peace with my name and my end. But it is the deeper truth that haunts me. It was not just that I convinced myself I had to do wicked things to survive," said the Baron, "it is that at times I enjoyed inflicting pain on others."

"Ah," said the Bogd Khan. "A man who has finally reached a point of honest witness to their ego, is a rare soul. Most men and women hide this darkest truth, pretending it does not exist. That deep within us, this seed of selfishness that enjoys destroying, that enjoys inflicting and witnessing the pain and suffering of others does not exist in them. You know enough not to be beguiled by the false morality of a world that calls a man evil for evil thoughts and praises another as good for saying and doing nothing. In recognising such truth you have freed yourself to a path of further healing."

"Look after Erdene," said the Baron. "Please help her understand why I had to say goodbye."

"There is no word we speak for goodbye as you mean it," beamed the Bogd Khan. "Only that I shall see you again very soon."

****

Chapter 17

Damdini Sukhbaatar was writing at a desk in his cell. A set of papers by his side, then he heard the click of the lock to the door. It swung open and Erdene stepped into the cell, with a look of resolute defiance.

"I was wondering when you would finally come," he grinned.

"Don't flatter yourself," she said coldly.

"So have you come to exact your revenge?"

"If it were up to me, you would have stopped breathing long ago," she said. "No. I have only come to tell you that a truly great and honourable man, who helped and protected our people has gone."

Erdene watched as the confidence of Damdini Sukhbaatar drained from him. She laughed.

"You of all people have nothing to worry about. He put Leonid Sipailov in charge with express orders that no harm come to you or any of your rat friends."

"Then why did you come to see me?"

"To remind you that you are a son of Mongolia," she said. "And if all of this ever means you are one day in power again, do not ever betray your people once more. Even if you are half the man he is, our future will be safe."

Erdene turned around and left the cell.

The Baron

Chapter 18

Vladivostok, Semyonov Headquarters, October 1922

The Baron stepped into a deathly quiet dimly lit room. He looked around until he heard the clink of a bottle dropping to the floor, to see the figure of a forlorn and drunk Semyonov half slumped against a wall.

As the Baron approached, Semyonov rubbed his eyes.

"Do not taunt me ghost," he moaned, before the Baron embraced him.

"You are not a ghost! It is really you!" declared Semyonov.

Semyonov stepped back, to look at the Baron.

"Yes, it is really you! We are saved!" yelled Semyonov, before embracing the Baron again.

"I can't save the Republic," said the Baron.

"Nonsense," replied Semyonov. "We have the Red God of War with us! You know every single Communist soldier is petrified of you. They sing songs to your downfall and even pray to be kept safe from you at night."

"General Eiche and the whole Soviet Army is on my tail. Vladivostok will be lucky to hold until the 12th of this month."

"Then why did you come?" asked Semyonov, rubbing his chin. "Ah, I get it now! You've come to save Mongolia and Erdene and condemn me."

The Baron shook his head negatively.

"Why does everything have to be about you Grigory Mikhaylovich?"

As the Baron spoke, Elmore Taggart appeared out of the darkness.

"Hello Semyonov," he said.

At first Semyonov looked pleased, before his face turned to anger.

"Snake! Betrayer!" he yelled as he launched himself at Elmore Taggart, before the Baron stepped in front to block his path.

"He is here to help you Grigory Mikhaylovich! Calm down."

"But the Americans are the reason the Republic is almost dead. They betrayed all of us," protested Semyonov. "You know their Wall Street completely finances and owns Stalin and the Communists? It is just another American corporation."

Chapter 18

"I don't have the time or inclination to stand here and be insulted," said Elmore Taggart. "Either you want a safe passage out of here, or not."

"Like Kolchak?" growled Semyonov.

"It is real Grigory Mikhaylovich," said the Baron. "You leave tonight and tomorrow you will be safe in the United States."

"It is true," said Elmore Taggart. "Let me tell you, you have one hell of a friend here. President Hoover didn't want to have anything to do with you, but the Baron understood the political sensitivities."

"What about you Roman Nikolaivich? Surely, you must be coming as well?"

The Baron laughed.

"You honestly think the United States could openly give sanctuary to the Devil?"

"No, I shall stay here and buy you some time, before I greet my admirers."

Elmore Taggart stepped over and embraced the Baron, before Semyonov did the same.

"Till next we meet," smiled Semyonov.

The Baron smiled as Taggart, helped Semyonov out of the room.

****

The Baron

The Baron, in thick arm chains, was led by an elite army unit of the Soviets, past a huge crowd of regular soldiers, to an awaiting train. As he passed by, soldiers crossed themselves and kissed and held out religious icons in front of themselves, as if to ward off contracting some kind of infectious evil.

Once at the train, the soldiers chained and padlocked the Baron into a solitary iron chair within an iron carriage, before closing and locking the door.

Chapter 19

Irkutsk, October 23, 1922

In a dark, dank cell, the Baron curled himself up as best he could to retain some body heat. Slowly the cell door opened to reveal the figure of Minei Gubelman.

"Minei, your still alive!" proclaimed the Baron. "Sorry, Yemelyan Mikhailovich. Or have you changed your name again?"

"Tomorrow Baron, you will face the justice of the people," said Minei Gubelman clinically.

"That is fine. I am ready. Why are you telling me? Don't tell me you are the judge?"

The Baron started laughing, causing Minei to growl.

"No one will believe anything you say, Baron. You are Lucifer, Satan and the Devil incarnate. The ultimate liar."

"Thank you for the compliments Minei," smiled the Baron. "No I will not embarrass you as the judge, so long as you run a half decent trial. You can do that can't you?"

Minei turned around and moved to the exit of the cell.

"You know you helped the Communists win the war more than anything don't you? grinned Minei. "We recruited hundreds of thousands of Christians and Jews upon the fearful exploits of the Devil and monster come to life as the Bloody Baron."

"One day people will know the truth Minei."

Minei Gubelman laughed.

"The people are too gullible and lazy and stupid to know the truth. They believe whatever we tell them to believe. This is the new weapon we have invented called the mass media. It doesn't matter how grotesque the lie, half the people believe it to be absolutely true and the other half know their life and future depends upon them pretending they believe it to be true."

"Even the greatest empires crumble Minei," smiled the Baron as Minei Gubelman huffed and left.

****

October 24, 1922

A windowless and largely featureless hall, except for the notable exception of a huge iron cage at its centre, and tables and chairs arranged around it.

Chapter 19

Inside the cage was the Baron, surrounded by a dozen elite guards. The rest of the chairs were occupied by Soviet party officials and army officers, who had come to watch the spectacle. An announcer appeared.

"All rise," he yelled. "The Court is now in session. Commander Yemelyan Mikhailovich Yaroslavsky presiding."

Into the room stepped Minei Gubelman, dressed in a perfect black suit and tie. He sat down at a long table, in between two other officials.

"Baron Roman Nikolai Maximilian von Ungern-Sternberg, you stand accused of committing more than 60 separate charges of atrocities, acts of barbarity and depravity," said Minei.

"So you say,"smiled the Baron. "Where is the evidence?"

Minei stomped a gavel and the room erupted.

"Order," yelled Minei.

"This is a court of law is it not?" asked the Baron.

Minei Gubelman nodded nervously.

"Then how can this be a true court of law if you plan to convict me on hearsay? Either this a mock court for show or a real court, which one is it Minei?"

More rumbling and yelling as Minei furiously bashed the gavel to regain order.

"Order," screamed Minei. "I shall direct the prisoner when to speak or when he is being spoken to."

"Then this cannot be a true court of law if you be both the judge and jury and executioner, can it?" yelled the Baron.

More rumbling and yelling erupted, as Minei struggled to regain control.

"Order," he yelled. "One more word and I will bar the prisoner from the proceedings and carry on in his absence."

The Baron shrugged his shoulders.

****

October 25, 1922

The Baron was returned to the same windowless hall, that had now been completely transformed. The iron cage had been replaced with an actual wooden prisoners dock, with a raised bench and table for the judge. There was even a cordoned off area with a jury of obvious military and party officials. Around the hall were oversize pictures of the heroes of the Communist

Revolution, including a huge picture of Lenin and now Stalin.

"All rise," yelled a court official as Minei Gubelman in judges robes appeared

"Will the accused please stand," said Minei.

The Baron stood up in the dock.

"We the court find the accused guilty of the crimes charged against them. I therefore sent-"

"Aren't you forgetting something first Yemelyan Mikhailovich?" asked the Baron.

Minei Gubelman stared at the Baron with complete contempt.

"The last words of the condemned maybe?"

"If you think you still have something to say to me," snarled Minei.

"Not to you Commander, said the Baron. "I have already forgiven you. I mean for the record to everyone else. "

Minei stuttered. "I suppose it is customary then. Does the condemned have any last words before I pass sentence?"

The Baron smiled and took a deep breath, as if a weight was lifted.

"If it pleases the court, I knew my fate was sealed the moment I surrendered."

The Baron

****

The Baron was led out to the back of the building to a courtyard and a set of posts in the ground. The back wall pock-marked with bullet holes. The Baron smiles.

"I do not fear death. Everything made of this world must eventually wither and die. But we are both of this world and not of this world and so nothing ever really dies."

****

The sound of a volley of shots echoed around the courtyard.

"I do not regret my life. Though I will never see old age, I feel I have lived in one lifetime more than anyone could possibly imagine."

****

Erdene with several monks walked through the dirty streets of the city to the Communist Party Offices.

The monks sifted through a pile of bodies in a pit, as Erdene held her mouth to fend off the stench. They find the body of the Baron, still with a smile on his face. They pull out the body and place it on a cart.

"I do not worry for my name or reputation after my body dies. People lie. I have seen men and women lie for all kinds of reasons, especially for their own survival. Therefore, I do not condemn those who came forward today and lied under oath to save themselves or their family."

****

A string of monks were singing and chanting as the body of the Baron was burnt on a funeral pyre overlooking the valley and Urga.

"Will I be remembered as some kind of monster? Maybe all that people will remember of me is the propaganda that I was some kind of Mad Baron, or Bloody Tyrant, the Bloody Baron."

****

Erdene in mourning dress, holding a vase of ashes leading a procession of Lamas. People lined either side of the road as the procession made its way toward the Bogd Khan standing on the front steps of the Palace.

The Baron

Erdene stopped in front of the Bogd Khan and handed the vase of ashes to him. He bowed to her and held up the vase before opening it in the wind, letting clumps of the ash out in short movements so that the ashes caught the wind and blew away.

"I do not care what those who did not know me, think of me in years to come. What matters is what those who did know me think and the truth in their hearts. Nothing is lost to the Universe. Everything yields but the heart. I forgive you."

www.ingramcontent.com/pod-product-compliance
Lightning Source LLC
Chambersburg PA
CBHW082247120626
46555CB00009B/2997